Wildwitch

Bloodling

Lene Kaaberbøl

Illustrated by Rohan Eason

Translated by Charlotte Barslund

PUSHKIN CHILDREN'S BOOKS

Pushkin Press

71–75 Shelton Street

London, WC2H 9JQ

Original text copyright © Lene Kaaberbøl, Copenhagen 2012
Published by agreement with Copenhagen Literary Agency, Copenhagen
Translation © Charlotte Barslund, 2016
Illustrations © Rohan Eason

Wildwitch: Bloodling was originally published in Danish
as *Vildheks: Blodsungen* by Alvilda in 2012

This translation first published by Pushkin Children's Books in 2016

1 3 5 7 9 8 6 4 2

ISBN 978 1 782690 86 3

Typeset by Tetragon, London

www.pushkinpress.com

CONTENTS

CHAPTER ONE

The Life of a Thirteen-Year-Old Girl

S he had been waiting for four hundred years. For four hundred years she had been staring through a transparent mass of solidified rock. It had trapped her body, her mind and her being for four long centuries. Her enemies considered this to be her grave, but she was still alive. Even down here there was life to be had – from time to time living creatures would scurry by, and she would snatch and devour them without mercy; mercy and compassion were qualities she had left behind long ago. Her anger had kept her alive.

Because she could feel it. She could tell what was happening outside, her wildsense screamed and writhed with the pain it caused her.

How dare they – these greedy little people with their roads, *their* houses, *their… now what did they call* them? Wires. Cables. Sewers. Bridges. Motorways.

Railway lines. *They carved deep, bleeding wounds through the wildworld; they ripped apart the delicate web of the wildways; they destroyed and they killed. Their roads, smeared with the entrails of dead and flattened animals, reeked of death. Forests and wetlands disappeared. Places where the wildforce had lived, breathed and reigned supreme for thousands of years turned barren and silent; all you could hear now was the banging and clanging of their unholy machines. Iron. Iron everywhere. Soon it would all be over – soon not even the strongest wildwitch would be able to mend the severed bonds.*

But now… now it might still be done, if only she could escape.

Her anger wasn't the only thing burning inside her. She could feel… no, impatience was too feeble a word. It couldn't begin to describe the fire that ravaged and scorched her core with every wasted second, every hour that passed without her getting closer to her goal. The time was now. *Not a day should be wasted. No more dithering, no more misplaced pity, no more caring about anyone or anything other than her one vital purpose: to break the hold of the stupid and the greedy, smash their web of death and* free *the wildworld.*

*It would take **everything**. Everything she had, every last vestige of power that she might coax, threaten, harass or bargain for. Desperately, she took stock of her strengths and despaired at her weaknesses. The weight of rock, the slow green power of plants, the mildness of the air, the soft energy of water, the warmth and deep life force of the Earth... even combined and united, they were not enough. She needed blood. Nothing else could win this battle that was already almost lost. Nothing else mattered – least of all... and her anger flared up more violently inside her when she thought about it... least of all the aimless life of a silly thirteen-year-old girl.*

Blood would open her prison. Blood would ensure her victory.

And then it happened. One drop fell. And then another. And then a third and a fourth.

More, *she screamed silently.* Give me one more drop!

It was as if she could see it quiver as it lingered in the air. As if it were fighting gravity, refusing to fall. But it did fall. And it kept on falling. And it landed.

YEEEeeeeeeeeeeeessssssssssssssssssssssss.........

She cried out in mute triumph. Her lips remained frozen; she was still trapped like an insect caught in a drop of resin a thousand years ago and now imprisoned in amber. But not for very much longer. She harnessed all her strength; she summoned all the wildness she possessed. Now. Now. Now!

The congealed mass of rock around her split. Cracks appeared and spread across its surface. In a roar of wildpower she straightened her body, hunched and bowed for four hundred years, and shattered her prison into smithereens. Solid rock boiled and turned molten once more; it burst and exploded; red-hot drops of melted glass sprayed the walls of the cave in hissing cascades.

Those greedy little people had no idea of what was coming. They had probably never even heard of Bravita Bloodling. But they were about to...

I sat up so quickly that I bashed my head on the bedside lamp. My heart was pounding and racing like a hurdler lagging behind the field, bang-bang-JUMP, bang-bang-JUMP; I looked around wildly as if Bravita Bloodling might be bent over my bed with outstretched claws and bloodlust in her burning eyes. She wasn't. The room was quiet and dark, except for a beam of moonlight that fell through the small, round window. On a mattress on the floor next to my bed my best friend Oscar was sleeping so soundly I could almost see a cartoon "ZZZZZ" above his head. No nightmares for him, that was for sure.

Easy now, I told my galloping heart, everything's fine...

And yet it took a long time before I was able to stop panting, and even longer before I could shrug off the feeling that my heart was trying to jump out of my body. Some of my previous dreams had already had too much in common with reality, and just because there was no four-hundred-year-old wildwitch lying in wait behind the battered bird books and old nesting boxes in need of repair, it didn't mean – at least my heart didn't think so – that I was out of danger.

But even if my dream had *some* reality in it – and that was a very big if, as most of my dreams were the usual mix of unreal and absurd, luckily – then Bravita wasn't trying to take my life, I reminded myself. She was after some poor thirteen-year-old girl and I was only...

My thoughts screeched to a halt. I looked at the old-fashioned, tick-tock alarm clock on my bedside table.

The luminous green hands both pointed almost straight up. The time was five minutes past midnight, and it was the last day of March.

Today, I would be thirteen.

CHAPTER TWO

A Cry in the Dark

I couldn't get back to sleep. I just skimmed the surface of sleep and I couldn't or didn't dare dive into it. Every time I was about to, my heart would start jumping hurdles again, and none of my attempts to reassure it worked.

Stop that. It was just a dream, I told myself.

Bang-bang-JUMP. Bang-bang-JUMP.

She's not here. She was never here. No one has seen her for four hundred years, and it really was a bit far-fetched to imagine she'd come back just to ruin *my* thirteenth birthday...

Stupid heart.

Eventually, I got up. I didn't turn on the light; there was no need to disturb Oscar. I carefully stepped over the duvet that almost covered his leg – three or four not very clean toes were sticking out from under the stripy duvet cover. Having nightmares tonight of all nights was ridiculous because everything was going really well – we were at my Aunt Isa's, Oscar, me, *and* my mum *and* my dad – and that in itself was a miracle. Tomorrow Kahla and *her* dad would be coming as would Mrs Pommerans, my aunt's wildwitch neighbour who had helped me a lot a few weeks ago when things were looking *seriously* bleak. Shanaia had sent a message with the kestrel Kitti, her new wildfriend, that she would visit, too. And The Nothing was here. Cat was currently off on one of his adventures, but had promised to be back around breakfast, and Bumble was probably sound asleep in his basket downstairs, snoring his doggy head off. I'd been allowed to have exactly the birthday I wanted, with all the people and animals I wanted. I'd been *so* excited about it that it really was ridiculous – ridiculous! – to get worked up over a silly dream.

I put on a pair of ragged old wool socks that served as slippers whenever I visited Aunt Isa. Aunt Isa had sewn a felt sole under each sock, so the cold wouldn't seep through when my feet touched the chilly floor. In an oversized T-shirt, bare legs and those woolly socks, I made my way quietly down the stairs and into the kitchen. By now it was quarter to four; I could tell the time from the clock above the kitchen table.

I opened the cupboard where Aunt Isa kept her supply of herbal teas. Many of them we drank purely because of their taste, but some had other properties. One or two might even calm a racing heart. I was a long way from understanding all of Aunt Isa's herbal remedies, but I had learned a bit. If only I could find... I studied the neat labels on tins and caddies until I spotted the two I was looking for.

Chamomile and valerian.

I turned on the hob and put the kettle on. Aunt Isa often used the wood burner in the living room, but I liked having a button I could press. The gas flame flickered blue and orange as it licked the bottom of the kettle and it didn't take long before it started rumbling. I fetched a mug from the hooks by the window and it was at that moment, just as I was turning back to the cooker, that I spotted something moving.

Outside in the darkness. A glimpse, just a glimpse of glowing eyes with vertical feline pupils.

"Cat?" I whispered softly.

But it wasn't Cat; I knew it the moment I uttered his name. Outside I could hear a low, singing yowl like the noise two alley cats might make when sizing each other up, only somehow... bigger.

I listened without moving. The water was boiling now, but the chamomile tea would just have to wait. Was there a feral cat out there in need of help?

I tried to peer through the window into the darkness, but could only see my own reflection. The golden eyes I'd seen were gone, yet the caterwauling went on. The animal – whatever it was – was still there.

If I opened the window, I'd be able to see and hear better. I lifted the hasps and pushed open the window, and a cool breath of night air smelling of rain wafted towards me. I leaned across the kitchen table, trying to see in the darkness.

At that moment a silent, grey-brown shadow came swooping towards me, a yellow beak, light-brown legs and clutching grey talons. I just managed to raise my arm in time so the big owl could land on it.

"Hoot-Hoot!"

Aunt Isa's wildfriend tilted his head and studied me. I wasn't sure that he liked what he saw. He'd never approached me like that before and, except for a few occasions when Aunt Isa had asked me to hold him – and he'd allowed himself to be held – I'd never been that close to him. He was big – by now I'd learned that he wasn't just "an owl", but a great horned owl. It meant that he was both rare and protected – though I don't think he was aware of it – and although I wasn't exactly scared of him, I maintained a healthy respect for talons, beaks and flapping wings. He too smelt of rain, and of wet feathers and blood, and the powerful talons now gripping my wrist had probably just taken the life of some poor mouse. But he turned carefully, without piercing my skin, hooting softly out into the darkness from which he'd just emerged.

The cat noise outside stopped. I heard something rustle in the bushes behind the apple trees, and then there was silence. All in all, none of this was any more peculiar than so many of the experiences I'd had when visiting Aunt Isa.

Except for just one thing.

I'd understood everything. I'd been able to feel the impatience of the cat screeching across my brain like a nail across a blackboard. And I'd heard Hoot-Hoot's warning, just as clearly as if someone had shouted it over a speaker system:

Go away, cat. You are too early. This is not the time.

"Clara. Did you let Hoot-Hoot in?"

I turned carefully so the owl wouldn't lose his balance.

"It looks that way..." I said.

Aunt Isa was standing in the doorway in her old dressing gown, which might once have been red, but was now a sort of faded pink.

"He's probably a bit confused," my aunt said. "I normally leave my bedroom window open, but..."

But that wouldn't be a good idea tonight. My mum and dad were using her bedroom, and Aunt Isa was sleeping on the sofa in the living room.

"... your mum probably wouldn't appreciate being woken up by a wet owl..."

Hoot-Hoot shook his wings, spraying us with pearls of rain. I couldn't help giggling.

"No, I don't suppose she would."

"But what's up with you, Clara? Couldn't you sleep?"

I shook my head.

"I had a strange dream. A nightmare, I guess you'd say."

Aunt Isa raised her eyebrows.

"About an animal?"

"No. No, I don't think it was about animals. Why do you ask?"

"Because you'll be thirteen tomorrow," she said. "Or rather... later today. It's a special birthday for a wildwitch and sometimes..." She hesitated as if she couldn't find the right words. "... Sometimes it brings with it special experiences or dreams about animals. But you said there were no animals in your dream?"

"No. It was... I think it was about... Oh, I don't know."

While we'd been chatting, the dream had quietly faded away. The details were gone. Someone had been very angry... someone had been trapped... someone had talked about blood. I wasn't keeping anything back on purpose; I genuinely couldn't remember anything very clearly now. My heart had calmed down and was beating normally again; I smothered a yawn.

"Looks like you won't be needing that after all," Aunt Isa said, pointing to the chamomile and valerian caddies.

"No," I said. "I think I might just go back to bed."

I raised my arm a little; Hoot-Hoot took off carefully and flew to his usual spot on Aunt Isa's shoulder.

"Well, good night again," Aunt Isa said with a faint smile. She checked the clock. "It's technically your birthday now, but I think I'll wait to wish you a happy birthday until the next time you wake up."

Birthday. Now why did that word make me more worried than happy? Hoot-Hoot looked at me with his orange-golden eyes, then polished his beak on his chest feathers.

This is not the time.

What did it mean? Had Hoot-Hoot even "said" that just as loud and clear as when Cat "spoke" to me? Or had I made up the whole thing because I was tired and hadn't had enough sleep?

I put the tea caddies back in the cupboard and returned to my room. I carefully stepped across Oscar, who was still lost to the world, crept into bed and slipped under my still-warm duvet. A few minutes later I was fast asleep.

CHAPTER THREE

Someone You're Happy to See

"You really have a way with animals, Isa. You must be something of a horse whisperer," my dad said. "Or rather, an owl whisperer... because if I'm not mistaken, then that's a great horned owl, isn't it?"

"Eh, yes," Aunt Isa mumbled with a rather guilty glance at my mum. "I'm... I'm just going to take him to the stable, so he can get some sleep."

Mum's lips tightened slightly, but she said nothing. And Aunt Isa did her very best to look like a completely normal woman who just happened to have "a way with animals". I could see she'd completely forgotten that Hoot-Hoot was perched on her shoulder; she was so used to it. Cat stretched and rubbed his head against my leg, and I got the distinct feeling that he was laughing at us.

Dad didn't know that Aunt Isa was a wildwitch. Or that I was one, well, *trying* to become one. And it was part of the big birthday agreement that we wouldn't talk about it.

I'd been pretty sneaky, you see.

I *desperately* wanted to spend my birthday with Aunt Isa so all my wildworld friends could be there. But I knew that Mum's reaction would be a flat no, if I just came right out and asked her.

Instead I started bringing up Aunt Isa whenever I visited my dad. I talked about her little stone cottage deep in the woods, about the meadow and the brook, and the animals, about Star the horse and Bumble the dog and so on. About Kahla, whom I'd got to know out there – without adding that she was Aunt Isa's wildwitch apprentice; about nice Mrs Pommerans who lived nearby – without mentioning that she was a wildwitch just as skilled as Aunt Isa.

Mum and Dad had been divorced for years and years, but they were still good friends and sometimes we would do things together like have dinner or go to the cinema. Especially now that Dad had a new job and was only a fifteen-minute bus ride away. It was nice that they got on so well. And because they actually saw each other quite often now, I knew it was only a matter of time before Dad would start talking to Mum about Aunt Isa.

"Clara seems really fond of her," he said one Sunday evening when he'd brought me back and stayed for dinner. "Why don't we invite her round for a meal?"

"Oh, she lives so far away," Mum said. "And it's difficult for her to leave all those animals."

I guess it's what you'd call a white lie. It was true that it took hours to drive to Aunt Isa's – but Aunt Isa could travel to our flat on the wildways in no time at all. But Aunt Isa only ever went on the wildways if she thought it was necessary, and it wasn't entirely safe, even for an experienced wildwitch like her.

"Well, then why don't we go to her?" Dad said. "I'd love to meet her, seeing as she's so important to Clara."

Yes! That was exactly what I'd hoped would happen. For a brief moment Mum looked as if she'd discovered a live frog in her mouth. Then she smiled.

"Yes, why don't we do that one day," she said. "When we're both free."

That was Mum-speak for forget-it-it's-never-going-to-happen. But I pretended not to understand.

"Brilliant!" I said. "I'd just *love* that. How about my birthday? I really want Aunt Isa to come and, like you said, it's difficult for her to leave the animals, so if we have it there..."

Mum shot me a look across the dinner table. A look that said I-know-exactly-what-you're-up-to.

"We can't just invite ourselves..." she began.

"But Aunt Isa said she'd be happy to have my party at her house..." I said.

"Did she?" Dad said. "How nice of her."

Mum had that frog-in-her-mouth expression again.

"I'm not convinced it's a good idea..." she said.

"Milla..." My dad placed his hand on top of one of hers, the one which was holding a fork. It looked a little bit as if he was trying to stop her from stabbing someone with it, but I think he just meant well. "Clara's not a little girl any more. Perhaps it's time she gets to decide how to celebrate her birthday."

Yes, yes, yes. Dad, I love you. On the inside I was dancing for joy, but I took great care not to look triumphant.

"It doesn't have to be a big, expensive party," I said, looking at Mum and hoping she would pick up the hint. "Just nice and quiet, and completely normal..."

"At your Aunt Isa's?" Mum sounded unconvinced. "I'm not sure how normal that's going to be..."

"Not everything has to be so conventional," Dad said. "I'm looking forward to meeting your sister. Come to think of it, it's odd that we've never met before..."

"Isa and I haven't seen a lot of each other since we drifted apart," Mum said, and heaved a sigh so deep that I knew that she'd backed down. I'd won! And yet the conditions were quite clear: no wildwitch tricks, in fact, nothing too bizarre could happen, and Dad must never know just *how* different Aunt Isa really was. It meant that The Nothing would have to move to the stable and promise to stay out of sight while Dad was around, and that was really sad because The Nothing *loved* parties and presents and cakes; but no one who saw The Nothing's ruffled, grey-brown bird's body and sad little girl's face could ever believe there was anything normal about her.

A pang of guilt made me get up.

"I'll take Hoot-Hoot to the stable," I offered.

"Thank you," Aunt Isa said. "And why don't you take a few scones for... eh, for Star and the goats."

I nodded, and grabbed a couple of freshly baked, just-buttered scones from the plate – not for Star, although Star was a cute little horse, but for The Nothing. Aunt Isa eased Hoot-Hoot onto my shoulder. Dad watched us and the owl with great interest.

"I can see why Clara likes coming here," he said. "I can think of few places where you get to befriend a great horned owl. And she's always been so fond of animals. Haven't you, munchkin?"

"Yes. I really... really like animals."

"More coffee?" Mum asked. "You won't be long, will you, Clara Mouse? We want to sing happy birthday to you."

The Nothing was sitting on a bale of hay, sniffling. Probably because it was a bit dusty here, which wasn't good for her allergy, but also because she was sad. Really sad, as it turned out.

"I brought you some scones," I said to cheer her up. She made no reply.

"Go on," I tempted her. "They're fresh out of the oven. Come get them while they're still hot."

She turned her head and looked at me with moist eyes. Her eyelids were thick and swollen, and the tears had left greasy trails down her cheeks and on her grey chest feathers. She sneezed.

"Happy birthday," she said in a forlorn voice.

"Thank you," I said, trying to act as if everything was fine. After all, this was the way it had to be. If Dad saw her – no, it didn't bear thinking about.

I put the plate down next to her.

"I have to go back to the house," I said. "They're waiting for me."

"Yes," The Nothing said. "I guess they are. All your friends." Her nose was almost blocked – when she said "friends", it sounded like "frebs".

"They're not all here yet."

"Aren't they? But they're bound to turn up. All the ones you like."

I couldn't help feeling a touch irritated, although I also felt bad for her, obviously.

"Listen," I said. "I'm really sorry you can't be there. I really am."

She just sniffed – a protracted, slurping snivel. It wasn't until I was halfway out of the stable door that she said something that must have been on her mind all along.

"You once told me that a friend is someone you're happy to see," she sniffed. "Now no one is allowed to see me. Does that mean you're not my friend any more?"

"No. Of course I'm still your friend!"

She sneezed again and a small grey-brown feather from one of her wings floated down to the stable floor.

"It doesn't feel like it..." she said.

CHAPTER FOUR

StarPhone

Mrs Pommerans arrived at three o'clock on the dot and greeted my dad warmly. Water was dripping from her floral raincoat and she wore one of those transparent plastic hoods you normally only see on very old ladies. There was something simultaneously good-natured and secretive about her, which made her resemble Cinderella's fairy godmother to a T.

"Happy birthday, Clara!" She kissed my cheek and gave me a present that turned out to be a small book about herbs.

"Is it time for presents?" Oscar asked.

"It looks as if we've already started," Aunt Isa said.

Oscar's present wasn't very big, but I could tell from his face that it wasn't just something his mum had bought – this was special. I squeezed it through the paper, but I couldn't work out what it was.

"Can I open it?"

"Of course," he said. "That's why I wrapped it up..."

It was a small, folding penknife, the length of my forefinger when closed and twice that when opened. The handle was pearly white with three shiny studs and the blade was slim and very sharp. It was an old knife that had once belonged to Oscar's grandfather. It was the knife we'd used many years ago when we mixed our blood for a blood oath.

"Oscar. But this is *your* knife," I couldn't understand why he'd want to part with it.

"I know. But Mum says... Mum says I'm not allowed it any more. It's not actually illegal, but she says that it..." He changed his voice to mimic his mum: "... *sends out the wrong message*. I was dumb enough to bring it into school to show it to Alex, and Ruler-Rita spotted it, had a fit and called Mum..."

Oscar's mother was tough. And she was a lawyer. Probably a bad combination if you were a twelve-year-old boy who wanted to hang onto his knife.

"And then I thought... it's better that you have it than it ending up in a skip. And I wouldn't have thought anyone out here worried about sending out *the wrong message*..."

I mulled it over.

"Thank you," I then said. "I really like it. But... I'm only borrowing it. If you want it back one day, all you have to do is ask."

Then my present from Mum and Dad was put on the table, and I forgot about everything else.

"Happy birthday, Clara Mouse!"

Even before I touched it, I knew what it was. I recognized the paper from the shop and the size of the box because I'd been there many times with Oscar, just to admire the wonder gadget and dream unrealistic dreams about presents. Or as Oscar would casually say when the shop assistant eyed us suspiciously and asked if he "could help us with anything", "Oh, we're just browsing."

Because it was way too expensive, the new StarPhone 3. There was nothing it couldn't do. It had GPS, mega games capacity, a subscription to StarMusic included in the price, memory like an elephant, it was *superfast* at everything and – thanks to StarSat's own global satellite network – you could get a signal anywhere. Star's ads showed mountaineers, polar explorers and people sailing around the world calling home to share their experiences from the remotest parts of the Earth. It had global coverage. "No more dark spots on the map" was the slogan they showed when the StarPhone's own catchy jingle played in the background.

The StarPhone 3 had only one minor flaw. It cost a fortune. And though I'd desperately wanted one, I'd never seriously expected to actually get it.

I heard a sharp whistle from across the table. A wide-eyed Oscar was staring at my present; he too had recognized the wrapping paper.

"Woooooooowwww..." he whispered in awe, and clearly had to restrain himself in order not to tear off the paper himself.

"Mum!" I exclaimed, as I demolished the wrapping. "You got it. You got it!"

Mum smiled.

"Yes. Happy birthday, sweetheart."

Aunt Isa put a steaming pot of birthday hot chocolate on the table.

"What was your present?" she asked.

"A StarPhone 3!"

"A mobile? How nice."

It was quite obvious that Aunt Isa hadn't a clue that a miracle had just occurred. A mobile... well, all right, I guess you could call it that. You could also say that a Ferrari was just "a car".

I clutched the wonder gadget and inhaled the sharp smell of new plastic and electronic circuits. My. Very. Own. StarPhone. And it wasn't the model 1 or 2. It was the one true, the only, the 3.

Cat jumped up on the table. The table wobbled underneath him. Cat is no lightweight; he's about the size of a labrador. First he sniffed the box suspiciously, then the phone and then he swatted my hand with a heavy paw. There was something... almost jealous about the way he did it. He swatted me again, this time with a hint of claw.

"Cat!"

Why do you need that, he said. *When you have me.*

The two couldn't be compared, I thought. Cat was... Cat. A wildfriend. Almost a part of me. I believed that I could hear some of his thoughts, and he had absolutely no problem reading all of mine. He guided me around the wildways, he looked after me – or he did when it suited him – and had taught me at least as much about being a wildwitch as Aunt Isa had. He had no reason to be jealous of a phone. Not even a StarPhone 3.

After being paralysed by shocks of joy and technological ecstasy, my normal brain activity kicked in.

"Mum, it's... please don't think I don't appreciate it, but... can we afford it?"

Mum ruffled my hair. "It's a joint present from Dad and me. But, yes, it knocked a big hole in the budget," she admitted. "On the other hand, you're only thirteen once and... well, this way we can at least keep in touch. Even when... you're here."

Then the penny dropped. This wasn't just a snazzy gadget that people from my school would envy.

"I really like it," I whispered. "And I promise to call you... all the time."

While I was still admiring my new phone, there was a knock on the door. Kahla and her dad were outside.

"Sorry we're late," Master Millaconda said.

Kahla was standing behind him, smiling cautiously, as if she had to remind herself how to do it. As usual she was wrapped in several layers of winter clothing in all the colours of the rainbow, and I knew that although the fire was crackling in the wood burner, and the rest of us were sitting around with glowing cheeks, she would keep at least one coat on. She'd never really grown used to what she called "the blasted cold" out here at Aunt Isa's.

"Doesn't matter," I said. "Shanaia's not here, either. I don't suppose you saw her?"

"No," Kahla said. "Happy birthday!"

"It's strange that she's not here," Aunt Isa said. "Because she sent Kitti with a message saying that she would be..."

"Kitti?" my dad said. "Is that another one of your friends out here, Clara?"

"Erm... you could say that. Though she's more a friend of Shanaia's." Also she was a kestrel, and my dad had actually met her once before, but there was no need to tell him that. Slowly but surely my neck and my jaw were starting to seize up from all the things I couldn't say.

Kahla gave me a book as well, and from Aunt Isa I got an amazing picture of Cat that she'd drawn herself. She's actually famous for her wildlife pictures, that's how she makes her money. But there was still no sign of Shanaia, and eventually Oscar, Kahla and I went outside "to check on the animals" – though what we were really doing was visiting The Nothing and bringing her some birthday cake.

"**O**scar, be careful!"

It was Kahla calling out, and I spun around to see what Oscar was doing.

He was making his way up to the roof of the stable. He must have jumped up onto the dry stone wall at the end of the stable, and now he was climbing up the uneven stones to the roof. He dug his fingers into the cracks where the mortar had crumbled and put his feet where the stones stuck out, so he looked like a smaller and more ordinary version of Spider-Man.

"Don't worry," he said, only slightly out of breath. "Everything's under control. After all, I *am* the school wall-climbing champion…"

Which indeed he was. He had the fastest time out of everyone at school on the climbing wall behind the sports hall. But that wall was made *specifically* for climbing, and you needed a rope and a harness before you were allowed to go on it.

"Get down," I said. "Before you break your neck."

He just flashed me a quick grin and carried on regardless.

"Boys..." I muttered.

"He's not bad, though," said Kahla, whose eyes were following Oscar's supple body.

"You know he's only doing it to show off, don't you?"

"Oh, yes," she said, never once taking her eyes off him. And it was at that moment I realized that Oscar was mostly interested in showing off in front of Kahla – and that she didn't mind at all.

I looked from Oscar to Kahla and back again. I felt a childish urge to cry: "But it's *my* birthday!" As if it were somehow unfair that not everything was about me. I got a very strange feeling in my tummy when I saw my best boy friend (not boyfriend!) trying to impress my best girl friend. Or my best and only wildwitch friend, at any rate.

He was high up now. So high that he would hurt himself really badly if he fell. But he didn't. He swung up his right hand and got hold of the ridge, and a few seconds later he was straddling the roof and flinging out his arms.

"I'm the master of the universe!" he shouted.

"Kneel, peasants! Kneel or you'll feel the full force of my power!"

I couldn't help laughing. You'd have to look long and hard to find anything less world-dominating than Oscar's freckled face. Even now when he was trying to look dictatorial and menacing, he still looked like someone who'd just remembered a great joke. He just didn't do serious.

Kahla, however, looked deadly serious, I realized. Almost... frightened. She was clasping her mouth with both hands and seemed hunched somehow, as if she was expecting someone to hit her.

"He's just messing about," I whispered. "He doesn't mean it."

"I know that," she said. "Do you think I'm dumb or something?"

Now it was my turn to take a step backwards. The look she gave me was just as dark and angry as the very first time I met her. Back then, she used to look down on me because I couldn't do much in the way of wildwitch tricks. Back then, she was annoyed and jealous because Aunt Isa chose to spend time teaching me how to be a wildwitch rather than devoting all her time to Kahla, the star pupil.

"What is it?" I asked. "Why are you so annoyed?"

But she just shook her head. "I'm not annoyed," she said. "You're the one who doesn't get it."

And she was probably right about that. I certainly didn't understand why she was acting like this. And on *my* birthday, too.

I put down the cake plate on the dry stone wall. Suddenly I had no wish to see The Nothing's sad, reproachful face, and even less of an urge to stand here arguing with Kahla.

"Where are you going?" Oscar called out from the ridge.

"Back inside."

"Wait. Why?"

"No reason. Why do I always have to have a reason? The two of you are free to come back in when you've finished playing..."

When I said the bit about playing, I wanted to make Kahla feel childish and maybe Oscar too, only a little bit. Unfortunately all it did was make me sound five years old, rather than thirteen and practically a grown-up.

"Aren't Kahla and Oscar coming?" Mum asked.

"They'll be back in a moment," I said and made an effort to look casual.

And in a way they were. Five minutes later Oscar did come rushing in, ashen-faced.

"Kahla's been bitten," he said.

"By what?" Aunt Isa asked.

"A leech, she thinks!"

CHAPTER FIVE

Mr Malkin's Present

Kahla was sitting on the dry stone wall and she wasn't looking at all well. Usually her skin was the colour of honey, but right now she was so white she could out-pale a corpse.

"I didn't feel anything at all," she said. "Not until now."

She had pulled up her trouser leg and on her calf there were five round, red marks. Something that looked like a black "Y" was at the centre of each.

"It does look like a leech bite," Aunt Isa conceded. "But you surely can't have got it here?"

"Don't you have leeches here?" Kahla said.

"Yes, but... not many that would bite humans. And certainly not on dry land. Because I don't suppose you've been wading up and down the brook, have you?"

Kahla shook her head and looked as if she were about to throw up. I felt sorry for her and bad that we'd argued. It felt silly now, especially because I couldn't have explained to anyone why we'd fallen out over a... well, a few stupid words, and I'm not sure Kahla could either. There were a lot of things in Kahla's life she hadn't told me much about, the most important being her mother. She had disappeared, that was all I knew, and no one seemed to know much else, and no one ever really talked about it. It meant that with Kahla, there were always shadows moving under the surface, somehow, and every once in a while I bumped up against all that hidden stuff, and Kahla's eyes would go dark and cold, like she couldn't help herself.

They weren't dark or cold now, just frightened.

"Is it dangerous?" I asked Aunt Isa.

"No, not normally." She placed her hand on Kahla's forehead. "You do feel a bit hot," she went on. "Let me sing some wildsong... eh, I mean, just let me, erm..."

Mum and Dad were watching. Kahla came to Aunt Isa's rescue.

"My dad can look after me," she said. "But I'd like to go home now."

Master Millaconda nodded.

"We *do* have quite a few leeches at home," he said. "They bite from time to time, but a thorough clean and a bit of rest tend to take care of it. Come on, Princess. We'll be home in a jiffy, I promise you. Can you put any weight on your foot?"

Kahla could.

"Goodbye," I said, and gave her a quick hug so she would know I wasn't angry any more. "Thank you for coming."

"Thank you for inviting us," she said, and the darkness and the anger were gone as if they were never even there.

W e'd hardly returned to the living room before Bumble jumped up and started barking. Not his big, scary go-away-or-I'll-tell-my-mum bark, which he used when he believed we were about to be invaded by something unwanted; this was three happy yelps and a lot of tail wagging. A friend was coming.

"It's probably Shanaia," Aunt Isa said. "Better late than never!" She went to open the door, and Bumble bounced and danced for joy as he tried to squeeze his way past her.

But it wasn't Shanaia.

"Malkin!"

"Hello, Isa."

"What a surprise..."

"A surprise? Surely tonight's the night young Miss Clara turns thirteen?"

"Yes, but... Why don't you come inside? Clara's parents are here, as is her friend Oscar."

"How nice," Mr Malkin said.

"Who is that?" Oscar whispered across the coffee table so loudly I was sure he could be heard all the way out in the hall where Mr Malkin was taking off his hat and coat.

"Mr Malkin helped me when..." I searched frantically for any other explanation than "when I passed my wildwitch trial with the Raven Mothers". "...Er, when I was ill," I said feebly. Mr Malkin was a part of Aunt Isa's circle of wildwitches, as were Mrs Pommerans, Shanaia and Master Millaconda. They helped each other with anything that was so difficult it required more than one wildwitch, and they met up four times a year to celebrate the festivals of the wildwitch year: Beltane, Lammas, Samhain and Yule.

Mr Malkin came into the living room, and I watched as Mum, Dad and Oscar all stared, no, it was more than that – gawped was probably the right word. Mr Malkin was a tall man with grey hair and he looked very old, but it was more likely to be the knickerbockers, the chequered golf socks, the silk waistcoat and the grey tweed jacket that made them stare so rudely, coupled with the fact that a mouse-like little rodent was twitching its pink nose in his waistcoat pocket. Mr Malkin looked like an extra from *Alice in Wonderland*.

"Hello, Miss Clara," he said. "And you must be Clara's mother?" He bowed politely and held out his hand.

"Septimus Malkin," he introduced himself. And Mum had no choice but to get up and say "Milla Ash. How nice to meet you," although I could see she was wishing him far away from the house and far, far away from me, my dad and Oscar.

My dad, too, had got up.

"Thomas Ash Twyford," he said. "Clara's father."

Oscar had eyes only for the rodent in the waistcoat pocket.

"Hi-my-name-is-Oscar," he reeled off to get the pleasantries out of the way. "And what's that?"

"It's a dormouse," Mr Malkin said. "I saved him from some crows and since then he more or less lives with me."

"Is he your wildfriend?" Oscar asked, oblivious to my desperate headshaking.

"He's wild and he's a friend," Mr Malkin said, "but not quite a wildfriend. At least not yet. He's still a bit young, so right now he's more in need of a foster parent."

"We'd better watch out or the owl will get him," Dad said with a smile.

Aunt Isa looked outraged.

"Hoot-Hoot would never even think of eating friends of the house," she said.

"A great horned owl with manners? I must say..." Dad mumbled. "You really do have a way with animals, Isa."

Mum's smile was becoming increasingly rigid.

"It was very nice of you to stop by," she said in a tone of voice which suggested that she was expecting Mr Malkin's visit to be short.

If he heard the undertones, he appeared to ignore them.

"Oh, don't mention it," he said. "It's an important day in the life of a young wildwitch. But more than that, an important night!"

"Night?" my dad said. "Why?"

Aunt Isa was waving her arms frantically behind my dad's back. My mum looked like she was going to be sick. Mr Malkin carried on, oblivious to them both.

"It's her Tridecimal Night, after all. It determines in so many ways the kind of wildwitch life she'll—"

"Malkin!" Aunt Isa interrupted him. "I'm so glad you're here. Because there was something I wanted to show you... outside."

Finally it began to dawn on Mr Malkin that something was wrong and that this party wasn't just another of those wildwitch get-togethers where it was completely natural for people to have animals in their pockets and discuss witchcraft as if talking about the weather.

He got up, although he had just sat down. But before he left, he stuck his hand into the pocket of his jacket – not the waistcoat, where the dormouse was still snuggled up – and took out a small object that he gave to me.

"Happy birthday," he said.

It was a small, yellowish-white disc with delicate carvings – a wheel with a hub at the centre and four spokes that divided the wheel into four quarters. It was carved from bone, I thought. A thin, round leather strap went through the hole so that I could wear it around my neck.

"You know that Isa, Agatha Pommerans, Shanaia, Master Millaconda and myself are great friends," Mr Malkin explained.

I nodded.

"In fact," he went on, "we're each other's witch-brothers and sisters. We form our own little witch-wheel, north-south-east-west with Isa as the hub in the middle. Together we can do more than we can on our own, and we can also call on each other, should we need help – even adult wildwitches need help every now and then."

He smiled as he said it, and yet I couldn't help shivering at the thought that there were dangers in the wildworld so great that it needed five fully grown wildwitches to take them on.

His long, slightly crooked fingers touched mine for a brief moment and a warm wave spread through my hand and up my forearm. I knew they weren't empty words – he'd given me another gift, one that couldn't be seen, but could easily be felt: a kind of blessing, I guess you'd call it. Sometimes the good wishes of a wildwitch have special powers.

"Until you find your own witchbrothers and sisters," he said, "then you may call on us. Not just your aunt, but on all of us. All you have to do is hold the wheel in your hand and shout: 'Adiuvate!' at the top of your voice. It simply means 'come to my rescue' in

Latin." His laughter lines deepened. "To be honest, I think it would still work if you just screamed 'help!' The Latin is more of a tradition. We'll hear you, no matter how you call."

"That's... really special," I said. "Thank you so much."

Mr Malkin just smiled, and then went outside with Aunt Isa. Mrs Pommerans also got up.

"I think it's about time I made my way home," she said. "Thank you for inviting me to your party, Clara. You take care now." She gave me a quick, dry peck on the cheek, put on her raincoat and went outside. I could see all three of them out there, Aunt Isa, Mr Malkin and Mrs Pommerans, who covered her hair with her transparent plastic hood because a fine drizzle of rain had started to fall. I could see that they were discussing something, and I wished I could hear what they were saying.

Dad, too, was looking out of the window.

"Tridecimal Night?" he said. "Wildwitch life? Witchbrothers and witchsisters?"

Mum gave a light shrug.

"Some of Isa's friends are a little... eccentric. Nature worship, Wicca and so on. That's why I don't want Clara to come out here too often."

"That doesn't mean they can't be decent people," Dad said. "He seemed like a kind and considerate man."

"Yes, I'm sure he is. But I don't want Clara tricked into believing all that stuff."

"Oh, Clara is far too sensible for that," my dad said with a smile. "After all, she's your daughter."

"Yes," Mum said and smiled with relief – probably because Dad seemed to have bought the idea that Mr Malkin was just some sort of friendly hippie.

I wasn't really listening. Through the window I could see Aunt Isa, Mrs Pommerans and Mr Malkin walk across the yard, down towards the bridge across the brook.

"He's leaving!" I was livid. "He only just got here and now he's gone. Mum, it's all your fault. Why couldn't you have been a bit nicer to him?"

Mum got up and she, too, followed the three figures with her eyes.

"I guess I could have been," she conceded reluctantly.

Dad looked from one to the other.

"Do you know what he was talking about, that stuff about the Tridecimal Night?" he asked my mum.

"Yes," she said, and my jaw dropped. "It's... I mean, some people believe... people like Mr Malkin believe that on the night a young person turns thirteen, they may be visited by an animal that brings them a task. It's a task they have to solve in order to grow up."

Her face had gone white. I mean, not just pale. Chalk-white, as if there were no blood left under her skin.

"Mum..."

"You might as well know it," she said to Dad in a very tense, flat voice. "My parents used to believe in that stuff. Isa still does."

"But you don't?"

"I want nothing to do with it," she said so sharply it sounded almost like a cry.

"But, Milla... is it really that bad? So bad that you can barely stand being in the same room as your own sister? Because I can see how hard it is for you to be here."

"You don't know what it was like..." she burst out. "You don't know what can happen... how badly things can go wrong... on a Tridecimal Night."

Something dawned on me.

"You've done it," I said. "You've had a Tridecimal Night yourself."

"Yes," she said. "And it was... terrible."

"What happened?"

She shook her head.

"Clara, I know you're fond of Aunt Isa. I know you like being here, and that you... and that you're fond of the animals. But you need to remember that not all animals are as cute and good-natured as Star and Bumble. Some animals are dangerous. A single blow from a bear's paw can kill you or a pack of wolves can tear you apart. Some animals are venomous. Some animals can give you diseases you can die from. *Don't you get it?*"

"Milla..." my dad said, putting his hand on her arm. "You do know that's a complete exaggeration, don't you?"

"Is it? *Is it?* You wouldn't know anything about that until you've seen... what I've seen."

Red. Blood red. Like meat in a butcher's shop, only it wasn't cut up neatly with a knife, but torn to shreds by teeth and claws. It. Because it was no longer a "she", no longer a human being, it was meat, the kind of fresh meat animals eat.

I can't normally visualize what my mum thinks. But this time an image jumped from her to me, though it was more than just a picture: my mum could also recall the smell. Suddenly I understood why she's never liked touching raw meat, and why we mostly ate vegetables, eggs and fish. It wasn't just because it was healthier.

"Who was she?" I whispered.

"What are you talking about?" my dad asked.

My mum said nothing. She just sat completely rigid and still, trying to keep her memories to herself.

"We're leaving straight after dinner," she said. "Before it gets dark. That's our agreement, and we're sticking to it. Do you understand?"

I looked at her white face and nodded.

CHAPTER SIX

The Accident

My birthday dinner ended up being a damp squib because Mum kept glancing at her watch, and I had a feeling she was watching every bite we took, to try and get us to chew faster. Aunt Isa noticed it too, but she didn't say anything. Oscar was the only one eating and chatting away, mostly about how super-cool my new StarPhone was and all the apps you could get on it, completely oblivious to the atmosphere.

"Thank you, that was a lovely meal," Mum said as soon as the last bit of ice cream had disappeared from our bowls. "It's been very nice, Isa, and thank you for having us. But I think we'd better get going now."

Aunt Isa looked pointedly at Mum.

"Are you sure?" she said, and I knew perfectly well what she was really asking: are you sure Clara shouldn't have a Tridecimal?

"Absolutely," Mum said. "Clara, go put our bags in

the car. Oscar, have you remembered all your things from upstairs?"

"Yes," Oscar said.

"Then we'll be off."

The road through the forest to Aunt Isa's house is pretty much a cart track, uneven, full of holes and crisscrossed by tree roots. You can't drive quickly – not unless you want the bottom torn off your car. And Mum knew it. But she still said:

"Can't we go a bit faster?"

Dad shook his head. We were driving his Volvo, not Mum's little Kia.

"Too risky," he said. "The road is just too bad."

The sun had already gone down. The darkness under the spruces was deep and impenetrable, but the sky above us was still more blue than black.

Oscar had borrowed my StarPhone and was trying it out.

"There *is* coverage," he said. "But it's taking ages to download."

I leaned back in my seat and looked out at the meadow to my left. At sunset I'd often seen deer there, and I thought I did see a ripple of movement, but it might just have been the wind ruffling last year's tall yellow grass.

Then I heard a loud crack from the forest. I just had time to turn my head and watch it happen.

"Look out!" Mum yelled. "It's going to fall!"

My dad hit the brakes so hard that the whole car shuddered and I was thrown forwards against my seatbelt. Right in front of our eyes a massive spruce leaned slowly further and further across the road and then suddenly came crashing down with a monstrous *thud* that made the earth ripple like a wave. The car skidded forwards another couple of yards, we heard the crunching of breaking branches, and then I couldn't see anything any more because the windscreen cracked and went white and opaque. In the same second I heard a pop as both airbags in the front inflated like balloons. Dad shouted something that sounded like: "Hold on tight!" But what was there to hold onto? Then a massive jerk went through the whole car, and once again I was hurled against my seatbelt.

The engine conked out.

There was total silence.

"Clara? Milla? Oscar? Are you OK?" Dad's voice sounded completely calm, as if just checking how things were.

"Yes," I squeaked.

"Yup," Oscar said.

"Milla?"

"I'm OK," Mum said. "I just got hit in the face by the airbag."

I'd never been in a car crash before. When cars crashed into something on TV there would be a loud bang and then a few seconds later the petrol tank would explode. Everything would go up in flames. I'd never imagined that the people inside the car would be speaking calmly to each other, almost as if nothing had happened.

"Shouldn't we be getting out?" I asked. "Before..." I didn't want to say "before the fire starts", so the word ended up hanging in the air.

"Just stay in your seats for now," Dad said. "Take a few deep breaths to get over the shock. Nothing is going to happen."

"Wow," Oscar said. "We crashed into a tree!"

He sounded as if he thought it was all super-exciting.

Dad opened his door. He had to give it an extra push and the hinges squealed, but he managed to open it. He got out.

If he was allowed to get out of the car, so was I. I unclicked my seatbelt and opened my door.

"Clara," Mum said. "First check if you're hurt. It's not always something you notice straight away."

"I'm fine," I said.

The front of the car had disappeared into the crown of the uprooted spruce. There were broken branches everywhere and a strong smell of resin and fresh wood. It was a strangely pleasant and Christmassy scent in the middle of what Dad called the "shock".

Mum and Oscar got out as well. Mum touched her nose, but there was no blood, so it looked as if we'd all escaped from the accident unscathed.

"We have to call someone who can clear away that tree," Mum said.

"Yes," Dad said. "But it's going to take time, Milla. And besides, the windscreen is a write-off. I think we have to accept that we'll be spending another night at Isa's."

Mum shook her head.

"No. We're going home."

"Milla..."

"We're *not* going back."

"Do you think it's better for the children to stay here? Milla, this could take hours..."

Mum looked around. The darkness had grown deeper and more night-like in just the ten minutes that had passed since the tree keeled over. And the temperature was dropping. I tightened my jacket around me, but could still feel that I was starting to get cold.

"I've found the nearest emergency rescue service," Oscar said proudly, waving my StarPhone. "Jasper &

Son, Auto Service and Windscreens, they're... hang on... twenty-four kilometres away. 24.6, in fact."

"Please could I borrow that thing?" Dad asked.

"Go ahead," I said.

Dad called, but could only get through to voicemail. It wasn't until his fourth attempt that he found a mechanic willing to pick up the phone after seven o'clock on a chilly March evening. I stood there shivering while he explained about the tree and the car and the Volvo's windscreen.

"What's the name of this place?" he asked Mum when he had finished talking to the mechanic. "I mean, which forest are we in?"

"I don't know. Why?"

"Because the mechanic said that it's the Forestry Commission's responsibility to move the tree. He'll only deal with the car. And besides, he can't get hold of a new windscreen until tomorrow morning. And he doesn't have a courtesy car we can borrow to drive all the way back to town. Milla, the only sensible—"

Mum looked around at us. At me, with my hands stuffed into my sleeves and my shoulders hunched right up to my ears, freezing. At Oscar, who'd started to shift his weight from foot to foot in order to restore some feeling to his toes. At Dad, who was still standing with one hand on the roof of the Volvo, looking tense and tired.

"Yes, I know," she said. "OK. Let's go back to Isa. I'm sure she'll know who to call to get that tree cleared away."

We'd been driving for about fifteen minutes when the accident happened, so it took quite a while to walk back. The darkness was encroaching upon us. Somewhere above us, an owl was hooting.

"Was that Hoot-Hoot?" Oscar asked.

"No," I said. "I don't think so. His voice is... deeper. Not so shrill. I think that was a tawny owl." Aunt Isa had taught Kahla to mimic six different owl cries, I remembered. She had taught me, too, but Kahla was better at it. When she did it, she *actually* sounded like an owl.

There was rustling in the blackberry tangle by the roadside. A branch snapped loudly under the trees where the darkness was as dense and black as oil.

"I'd completely forgotten how alive a forest is," Dad said. "Even at night. Or rather, *especially* at night."

"Yaooooooooowwwwwwwwwr."

It was as if the forest answered: a long, low, feline sound. I had a flashback to the cat outside the kitchen window and Hoot-Hoot who had made it go away before I'd had a proper look at it. *You are too early. This is not the time.*

But was it time... now?

A supple movement and a silent jump. A flash of moonlight in bright eyes.

Something appeared on the road in front of us, seven or eight metres away at the most. A tall, slim cat with its mouth half open and its front paw raised, glossy, almost silver in the moonlight, though I suspect it would have been more... lion-coloured by day.

It stood very still and stared at us. Its ears were standing straight up and they had long, furry tufts that quivered attentively.

"A lynx!" Dad exclaimed, as if he couldn't believe his own eyes. "It's a lynx! Stand very still... It'll go away in a—"

Mum didn't stand still. She charged towards the lynx while waving her hands in the air as if trying to shoo away a horse.

"GOAWAY!" she shouted. "Goaway – goaway – goaway!!"

The lynx hissed and the moonlight glinted on its fangs. Then it leapt across the road, into the bushes and the dry grass.

I stood rooted to the spot with my mouth hanging open for several seconds. Not because of the lynx, exciting though it was. But because of Mum.

My mum was a wildwitch.

There could be no other explanation.

The way she had shouted **GOAWAY**... it sounded completely like when I did it. The only bit of wild-witchcraft I'd ever been any good at... I'd inherited from my mum.

"Mum!"

She spun around. She stopped staring after the lynx and looked at me instead. I'm sure she realized that she'd given herself away. That I knew exactly what she'd done, and how she'd made the lynx disappear. But she acted as though nothing had happened.

"A lynx," she said. "Around here? I wonder if it could have escaped from the zoo."

"It's possible," Dad said. "Why else would it be so ready to approach people? But I don't think trying to scare it was very wise, Milla. Threatening it like that... what if it had attacked you instead of running away?"

"But it didn't," my mum said. "Come on. Let's get back to Isa's so we can warm up. I've had enough wilderness excitement for one night, thank you very much."

"Mum..."

"Not now, Clara."

She started marching down the road. We followed. Oscar was bouncing with excitement.

"First we drive into a tree," he said. "And then we're attacked by a lynx. Wow, that's *so cool*!"

"We weren't attacked," I protested. "It was only..."

"Oh, don't spoil it," he said. "A big, super-cool, scary *lynx*!"

CHAPTER SEVEN

Those Who Walk Blindly Through Life

Bumble was thrilled to see us again. Aunt Isa was more apprehensive.

"What happened?" she asked.

"A tree fell across the road," Dad said.

"Right in front of us," Oscar clarified. "Isa, we drove straight into it!"

"Goodness me. Was anyone hurt?"

"No," my mum said. "Isa, please let's go inside where it's warm."

Because Aunt Isa was still standing in the doorway, almost as if she were blocking it deliberately.

She looked at my mum. Then she shrugged her shoulders in a strange well-you-asked-for-it way.

"All right then, in you go," she said.

Inside the living room, The Nothing was sitting in her favourite chair with a book. On the coffee table in front of her was a pot of tea and two steaming cups, one with a straw. The Nothing had no arms, only wings, and where a bird would have had talons, she had soft fingerfeet, which could indeed grab things, but made it hard to walk. When she sat on her bottom with her short legs stretched out, she could hold the book in one fingerfoot and turn the pages with the other, but she struggled to reach her own mouth. The straw made it much easier for her to drink.

When she spotted my dad, she dropped the book.

"Oh, no. Oh, sorry. Oh dear, oh dear! I'm not here... I'm not here at all..." She took off on clumsy, grey-brown wings and flapped through the living room towards the kitchen, so flustered that she dropped a blob of very birdlike poo on the rug and then sneezed in sheer confusion. "Achoo. Oh dear, oh dear, oh dear..."

"You can come back," Aunt Isa said. "He's already seen you."

My dad looked gobsmacked. Uprooted trees and crashed cars he could handle, and he'd even taken the lynx in his stride, but The Nothing... there was no way he could fit The Nothing into his understanding of the natural order of things.

And no wonder. She wasn't a bird, and she wasn't a human being. She was what's known as a chimera, a cross between two living creatures, not born in the usual fashion, but created through blood-art and magic. She was an experiment gone wrong, a mistake. A nothing, useless and worthless, at least if you'd asked Chimera, the only "mother" The Nothing had ever known. She couldn't fly very well, she had no beak nor a mouth filled with sharp shark's teeth like her more successful sisters, just a soft and open little girl's face in the middle of her ruffled plumage.

But though The Nothing still had no other name than the one her so-called mother had given her, she wasn't nothing. She kept practising, and she was getting better at doing the things she could do. She loved helping out and got very excited at every little task she accomplished because it made her feel that she was something, that people needed her. And if my dad said anything at all that might hurt her feelings, then I would... then I would...

He didn't say anything. He picked up his jaw and managed to close his mouth, but he still couldn't stop staring.

The Nothing stopped flapping around and executed a clumsy and inept landing on the coffee table, making the tea service clatter perilously.

"Sorry," she said again.

"You don't have to say sorry," I said firmly. "If anyone should apologize then it's us. We

should never have hidden you away. I really, really wanted you to come to my birthday, and luckily there's still time. Dad, this is The Nothing. She's my friend."

"*Am* I?" she exclaimed joyfully. "Oh, thank you. And I'm your friend too. Again. Definitely! For ever and ever. Hello, Clara's dad. I'm very pleased to meet you." She couldn't shake his hand, but she performed a surprisingly neat little bow.

"Er... good evening," Dad said. "I'm... I'm pleased to meet you too."

At that moment I wanted to give him the biggest hug in the world. I was totally aware that he had a zillion questions – where did she come from, who was she, how could she exist at all. But he didn't ask any of them. In fact, he succeeded in directing his eyes away from what for him was an impossible creature and fixing them on Aunt Isa instead.

"I'm sorry that we've come back unannounced," he said. "But it doesn't look like we'll be able to drive back tonight. I'm hoping you know someone we can call to clear away the tree?"

"I know who that is!" The Nothing chirped happily. "It's on a piece of paper... erm, right there." She pointed the tip of her wing at a chest of drawers. "In the little green book, second in the pile to the right."

"The Nothing keeps track of things around here," Aunt Isa said. "I don't know what I would do without her."

The Nothing straightened up and beamed proudly. "*And* I can read," she said.

Dad borrowed my StarPhone again, this time to ring "Andy the Forester", as Aunt Isa called him. It suddenly occurred to me that so far Oscar and my dad had made much more use of the phone than I had. Don't get me wrong, I was over the moon to have got it, but I was starting to realize that I would be more excited about showing it off to the girls at my school than actually using it. This surprised me because when I'd been desperate to get one, I'd been convinced that I'd be using it for absolutely everything. But right now it was obviously better that Dad could call "Andy the Forester" without having to go outside and climb the hill behind Aunt Isa's house to get even a bit of a signal, like we normally had to. Instead he went to the kitchen and closed the door. Perhaps so he wouldn't stare at The Nothing the whole time, but I think mostly because he didn't want Mum to interfere.

Mum was standing by the window, looking out into the darkness. She'd folded her arms across her chest and looked like she was hugging herself.

"Was that you, Isa?" she asked.

"What do you mean?"

"Did you make that tree fall over?"

"Seriously, Milla… do you even believe that yourself?"

Mum turned around.

"It's just that this suits you to a T, doesn't it? You didn't want us to leave. You wanted Clara to have a Tridecimal Night."

"Yes," Aunt Isa said very calmly. "I did want that. Whether you like it or not, Clara is a wildwitch, and it's hard for a wildwitch to know which path to choose if she hasn't had a Tridecimal. Clara is almost grown up. She should be allowed to decide for herself. It's her life we're talking about."

Something ominous flashed in Mum's eyes, and I could see that she was very, very angry.

"You've hit the nail on the head," she said. "Clara's *life*. Which I take care of, and which you seem to be willing to risk."

"Mum…" I ventured cautiously. "Aunt Isa takes care of me too. She just does it a bit differently from you…"

"Whatever you might think," Aunt Isa said, "I definitely didn't make a tree fall down several kilometres away simply to get my own way."

"You want me to believe it was a coincidence?"

"Perhaps it was. Perhaps not. Sometimes the wildworld makes sure that what *needs* to happen, happens. Or at least, is given the chance to happen. The rest is up to us. But one thing I do know: those who walk blindly through life are no safer than those who look where they're going. Quite the opposite."

They stared hard at each other for a very long time. It was as if they'd forgotten that Oscar, me and The Nothing were also in the room. Oscar looked wide-eyed from one to the other, and for once he stayed quiet. Right now I thought that my mum and my aunt resembled each other more than ever. It wasn't about their clothes or hair – Aunt Isa still looked like a proper wildwitch with her long plaits, her lumberjack shirt and her worn green gardening trousers, while Mum was a thoroughbred city woman with her neat, short bob, classic Breton top and black skirt... chic and smart, even if her tights were now laddered. But there was an expression in her eyes, the way she was standing, a sense of... hidden forces. My mum mightn't be as much of a wildwitch as her big sister, and she'd kept both herself and me away from wildwitchery for many years. She did not want to be a wildwitch, and still less did she want me to be one. But she couldn't escape it. She had the power. Only she'd used it to protect me all these years – keeping me away from something that terrified her. No wonder she and I both excelled at screaming **Goaway!** at wild animals.

"Mum," I said. "If you don't tell me what happened on your Tridecimal Night – how will I ever know if I want one?"

My heart was beating almost as erratically as when I woke up from my nightmare last night. Aunt Isa was clearly of the opinion that a Tridecimal was massively important, and so was Mr Malkin. Right now, I didn't know who to believe.

Mum looked at me for a long time. Then she shook her head.

"No," she said. "I don't want to put you through that. It's enough that you know it's dangerous, so I'm saying no. I won't let you. We'll stay here tonight because we have to. But you're not going anywhere, do you hear me? You won't be stepping outside. You won't even go near the window after midnight."

And it was clear she thought that was the end of the matter. I wasn't quite so sure.

CHAPTER EIGHT

Tridecimal Night

For the second night in a row we got ready to go to bed in Aunt Isa's house, but Mum swapped everything around. She carried my bed linen down from my room upstairs and made my bed on the sofa in the living room. Dad and Oscar slept in my room. Aunt Isa got her bedroom back, and The Nothing no longer had to sleep in the stable, but settled instead on her usual perch next to Aunt Isa's worktable, her face tucked under her wing. She looked her most birdlike when she was asleep.

"And where will you be sleeping?" I asked Mum.

"Nowhere," she said as she flopped into one of the armchairs in the living room and threw a blanket over her legs. She'd made coffee and taken her keys out of her handbag. She held them up so that I could see them. "I learnt this trick at the newspaper when I was a trainee on night shifts. I've no intention of going to sleep even for a second tonight, but if I do doze off, I'll drop my keys and the sound will wake me up."

Aunt Isa looked at both of us, but I think she could see there was no point in any further discussion.

"Good night, Milla. Good night, Clara."

"Good night, Aunt Isa."

Mum said nothing. She just pointed at me with the hand that was holding the keys.

"Lie down."

I did as I was told. It felt weird lying there, trying to fall asleep, while she was sitting next to me awake. As if I were ill. Or a baby. It wasn't even very late, it had only just gone ten o'clock, but I'd slept so little the night before that my eyelids soon began to close.

I *t is time.*

Was it a thought, a voice or a dream? I don't know. All I know is that something inside me quivered and sang, like when you pluck a guitar string.

I opened my eyes.

Mum was still sitting up straight in her "guard chair" with her keys in one hand. But I could see right away that she was asleep. The hand with the keys was resting in her lap and her head had lolled to one side. The coffee in front of her had stopped steaming long ago and was probably stone cold.

Cat was standing by the door to the passage. He seemed even bigger than usual and he fixed his unblinking yellow eyes on me.

Come.

I have four pale scars on my forehead, one for each of Cat's claws, where he scratched me the very first time we met. Where he scratched me – and lapped up my blood with his rough pink tongue. The scars have faded so they're barely visible; one especially has almost disappeared, and they stopped hurting ages ago. But just at that moment, I couldn't help touching them.

"I don't know if this is what I want," I whispered.

He made no reply. He just turned around and disappeared. I'm deliberately not saying that he went "out" because the door was still closed. But Cat has his own way of using the wildways. He can disappear in seconds without leaving anything behind but a small cloud of fog.

It was his way of saying "suit yourself". But I suddenly knew without it being said that if I didn't follow him now, I'd never see him again.

The thought seared through me. Would he really leave me unless I followed him?

"That's really mean of you," I whispered. "You can't do that! You're supposed to be *mine*."

There was no reply, and deep down I knew it wasn't true. Cat wasn't mine, he never had been.

It was the other way around. I was his – and if he wanted nothing more to do with me, there wasn't a lot I could do about it.

Carefully, I got up. Mum didn't stir. Was it Cat who'd made her sleep like that, even though she'd made up her mind not to? I didn't know. The truth was, I knew very little about what Cat could or couldn't do.

I couldn't walk through closed doors or walls like Cat, so I had to open the door to the passage very quietly in order not to wake Mum or The Nothing, who was still fast asleep with her head under one wing.

Now. It is time.

Once I'd started moving, I couldn't stop. The *now* feeling was so compelling that I didn't wait to put on my boots. I just opened the door and stepped outside, and I didn't even feel the cold. The wind grabbed at my T-shirt and my hair, but I wasn't cold. I walked across the yard in bare feet, and I couldn't feel the pebbles I trod on or the chill from the ground.

Now.

The forest was alive. The sky was teeming with birds, the bushes were rustling, the grass on the meadow rippling, and something was splashing in the brook. The moon hung round and huge above the hill behind Aunt Isa's house, and in the very near distance something that wasn't an owl or a lonely dog was howling. The wet grass brushed my ankles, and it felt almost like a kiss.

I went down to the brook because I knew that it was there, on the border of Aunt Isa's wildward, her own little witch's dominion, that they were waiting for me.

My heart was beating wildly, but not because I was afraid. I don't think I can explain the feeling that was surging inside me – as if every twig snapping in the forest meant something, as if the wind whispered words I could almost understand, as if everything suddenly had meaning, and that I was *meant* to be here now, not yesterday or tomorrow, but right here and nowhere else at this one precise moment in time.

The lynx was standing on the other side of the bridge. It watched me calmly with its golden eyes, and its ears with their dark tufts of hair were standing straight up. I wasn't surprised to see it.

But it wasn't alone. The moment I put my foot on the bridge, there was a rush in the air above me, and a cloud of birds flocked around me so densely that I had a flashback to Chimera's furious shark birds. But this time there were no teeth snapping and tearing at me. My hair whipped across my face in the whoosh from a thousand wings: great tits, oystercatchers, partridges, wrens, rooks, blackbirds,

greylags and seagulls, a falcon, a common buzzard, three owls, a flock of sparrows, birds that belonged here and birds that definitely didn't, seabirds and woodland birds, mountain birds and wetland birds, predators and sparrows together.

And not just birds. Below me the brook was seething with fish and aquatic animals, a family of six otters wiggled across the bank towards my feet, and a pungent and unmistakable smell of fish-breath and water weeds wafted towards me.

"Uiiiiih, uiiiiih, uiiiiih," they squealed in excitement, and the otter at the front planted a wet front paw on my bare foot and looked up at me with a kind of otter smile, so I could see the glistening white fangs in its lower jaw and its pink tongue.

More animals came pouring in from the meadow and the forest: spotted sika deer, small roe deer, bigger fallow deer, a herd of red deer led by a huge stag with twelve-point antlers, hares and pheasants, water voles and polecats, red pine martens and two broad badgers, at least eight foxes, their tails proudly in the air, a dark-brown wild boar with coarse bristles and three sows by his side, a vast tribe of wild goats, too numerous to count...

Then the goats parted and I saw something enormous and dark cutting through the flock like an icebreaker through thin ice. Its back sloped up towards massive, hump-like shoulders, its head was so wide I don't think that I'd have been able to reach around it with both my arms. Its horns were sharp, but it was the broad forehead and powerful neck and shoulders that instilled respect. Its fur hung in matted clumps and the eyes watching me were tiny compared to the rest of this giant beast.

A bison. It was a bison bull.

It stopped next to the lynx and pawed the ground with its front hoof a couple of times, but not as a threat. And the lynx stayed calmly next to the giant bison.

Then I could hear howling again, closer and sounding more like barking. A dozen or so loping figures with amber eyes, broad paws and panting jaws half-open appeared from the forest. The wolves had arrived.

A mouse darted up my leg, a small, grey house mouse I was almost sure I'd seen before. It climbed all the way up to my neck and perched on the neckline of my T-shirt, so I could feel its tiny, delicate claws against the skin on my collarbone.

There was a buzzing and humming and bustling of insects all around us – flies, beetles, gnats and heavy-winged moths; a winter-clumsy bumblebee flew right into my cheek with a hairy bump, but it didn't sting me.

It was as if all the wildworld's living creatures that could come had done so. Some must have used the wildways; others had probably wandered for hours or days on nature's more usual paths. And all of them, every single one of them, was looking at me. Golden eyes, dark eyes, tiny eyes and huge deer eyes, yes, it seemed as if even the multifaceted insect eyes – with or without stalks – were following every single move I made, every breath I took. They were like a weight, all those gazes; the air grew thick and heavy like water, and I knew that they were waiting for something.

Breathing became harder. My heart was now pounding so loudly my ears were roaring. What did they want from me?

I could make them go away. I could scream at them. I was good at that. And then I'd be able to breathe again.

But that wasn't why I was here and certainly not why they had come.

Suddenly it seemed to grow lighter. A trail of fire crossed the sky above us, and I felt a warmth and a laughter inside me which wasn't my own.

The time has come, little wildwitch. Time for you to show who you are.

It was the firebird. At once real and magical, natural and supernatural. Its wings were blazing, its burning tail glowed and was reflected in all the animals' eyes as fiery orange pinpoints. Once before, back when I'd undergone the Raven Mothers' trial by wildfire, it had enclosed me in its flaming wings and asked me who I was. Now it had returned, as if it wanted to make sure that what I had said back then, in the heat and the fire, was still true.

The otter nipped at my trouser leg.

"Uiiiiih. Uiiiiih." Its eager squeal cut through the otherwise deafening noise of thousands of animals snorting, breathing, scraping, raising their tails, sweeping their antlers, grunting, pushing, flapping or stamping. In a way there was silence – apart from the otter, no one roared, screeched or howled – but so many living creatures can't be together in one place without even their silence being noisy.

Carefully I put my hand on the mouse on my shoulder. It jumped up and settled in my palm, rubbing its nose with the little front paws that almost looked like hands.

"OK," I whispered. "Have it your way." I looked around, trying to meet as many eyes as I could. "Yes. Whatever it is you want, then yes. I promise to try!"

They kept looking at me. I got the distinct feeling that trying wasn't good enough.

I took a very deep breath. Closed my eyes for a moment. *Sensed* them with all of my wildsense, which wasn't my eyes, ears or nose.

"Yes," I said quietly once more. And then, at the top of my voice: "YES!"

The noisy silence returned for a moment.

Then they all set in motion, almost simultaneously. The bison bull snorted, shook his massive head, turned around and left. The flocks of birds took off and scattered. The herd of deer set off with a jolt, so all you could see of them in the darkness were their bouncing white rears, each with three black stripes that made them look like they were all wearing licence plates with the same number – III.

The otter family squeaked contentedly and flipped themselves back into the brook, and within minutes there were no more insects around than there usually would have been on a cold spring night in April, that is, hardly any. Above us the firebird laughed and danced its blazing trail across the sky until I couldn't see it any more.

The mouse remained in my palm. Other than that, the lynx was the last to leave, moving off in long, soft, feline bounds that took it into the darkness under the trees in a matter of seconds.

Suddenly I could feel the sharp, icy gravel of the road under my feet. The wind cut through my T-shirt, raising a trail of goosebumps across my bare arms.

"I promise," I said to the mouse. "But I might need a bit of help from you all."

It twitched its whiskers, rubbed its nose again, darted up my arm and down my back until it could safely jump to the ground. When I turned around, it was gone.

Mum was standing a little further down the drive. She'd come outside without a coat and without swapping the slippers she'd borrowed from Aunt Isa for outdoor shoes. She was standing very still, her arms hanging limply down her sides, and I knew she must have seen some, if not all, of what had happened.

She's going to tell me off, I thought. She's going to be so mad at me, madder than she has ever been.

But she wasn't.

She just looked at me, her face blank and devoid of expression. She didn't even look scared any more. It was as if the worst had already happened, so there was no reason to get worked up over anything else.

"Do you even know what you've promised to do?" she asked.

I bit my lip. I was starting to shiver from the cold now, and my feet were completely numb.

"No," I said at length. "But I couldn't do anything else."

That wasn't true. I could have made them go away. But if I'd done that, I'd never be a proper wildwitch.

That was why Cat had threatened to leave me. Half-hearted attempts were no longer enough. It was all or nothing: either I was committed with all my heart, or not at all. I could have done what my mum did. I could have turned my back on the wildworld and used all my energy to keep it at bay, so my life could carry on all nice and normal. Only I couldn't bear that. Because if there was one thing I now knew with greater certainty than ever before, it was that *yes* – I did want to be a wildwitch.

CHAPTER NINE

The Puma

I have to go now.

It was Cat's voice in my head, but I was so soundly asleep I didn't seem to be able to wake up properly. Besides, Cat always came and went as he pleased anyway.

"Mmmmh."

Then my drowsy brain realized that he didn't normally warn me before he disappeared.

"Cat?"

We'll meet again. But not until you really need me.

"What?"

Go back to sleep. But don't forget this.

I didn't have much of a choice. Sleep opened up underneath me like a black hole and I fell into it.

W hen I woke up next morning, I was stiff and sore all over, as if someone had been pummelling me with their fists all night. Cat. Where was Cat? He'd told me he would leave unless I went to meet all the animals that were waiting for me, and I'd done it. So why had he left me anyway?

At least he'd promised to come back. I tried to be content with that.

Bumble came up and sniffed me thoroughly from head to toe, clearly of the opinion that I smelt strange but interesting. I crawled off the couch and went to persuade Aunt Isa's somewhat temperamental water heater to give me a hot bath.

When I reappeared in the kitchen with wet hair and wearing one of the bath towels as my dressing gown, Aunt Isa was making tea. She put down the kettle and looked at me.

"So tell me," she said.

I didn't know where to begin.

"Mum fell asleep..." I said tentatively. "And Cat came... and... and... if I hadn't gone with him, then..."

Aunt Isa nodded.

"I had a feeling. I wasn't sure, but even ordinary wildfriends don't bond so closely with humans who don't want to be wildwitches. And if you refuse your Tridecimal..."

"Then you'll never be a *proper* wildwitch," I said quietly. "I understand that. And he would have left me. He would have abandoned me." And not promised to come back...

"Yes," Aunt Isa said. "He probably would have. So who was it? Was it the lynx?"

"No. Or rather, yes. The lynx was there as well. But..." How could I explain? All those beaks and wings and paws and hoofs and horns and claws and *eyes*, especially the eyes...

"Let me see," Aunt Isa said, cupping my face with her hands and looking into my eyes.

... partridges, wrens, rooks, blackbirds, greylags, gulls...

... sika deer, roe deer, fallow deer, red deer, hares and pheasants, water voles, red martens...

Bison. Mice. Otters. Wolves.

The firebird.

The lynx.

Aunt Isa let go of me. She rubbed her hands against her own cheeks a few times, and for once she looked at a loss.

"Not just one animal," she whispered. "Or one pack or one flock."

"No."

"But how... I mean, normally an animal wants your help. It wants something. One of its chicks might have fallen out of the nest, or its home has been destroyed and you need to help it find a new one, or it's threatened by some illness. Once you've worked out what it is and solved the task, then you've passed your Tridecimal. Then you're essentially a fully-fledged wildwitch, even though you might still have a lot to learn."

I nodded. That much I'd understood.

"But how come... all those animals... how can they all have the same problem? What on earth are you supposed to help them with? I've never heard of a case like this before."

I stared down at my hands. I don't really know why, maybe I was just as confused as Aunt Isa. I thought that I ought to do something, only I didn't know what.

"Isn't there anyone we can ask?" I said.

"The Raven Mothers. We can always try them. Normally it's part of the test to find out what the task is about, but... this isn't a normal Tridecimal test. If your mum will let you, we could go to Raven Kettle today."

"I don't think she'll be too happy about it," I said. "But... Aunt Isa, she's not in charge. That was one thing I learned last night. In order to become a good wildwitch, I have to do what *I* have to do. Even if my mum says no."

Aunt Isa straightened up at that moment and the floorboards behind me creaked a little. I could pretty much guess what had happened. When I turned around, Mum was standing in the doorway. She'd heard what I'd said.

Her eyes looked darker than usual.

"Come here," she said.

"Where are we going?"

"Out. Anywhere just as long as no one else can hear us."

Aunt Isa raised her eyebrows, but she didn't say anything.

"I just need to get dressed..."

"Yes. Meet me in the stable when you're ready."

"But... why?"

"You asked me what happened on my Tridecimal. Perhaps I should have told you yesterday, but I was hoping... anyway, I didn't tell you. But if you want to be in charge of your own wildwitch life now... then you need to know what you're signing up for."

She threw a last, dark glare at Aunt Isa – I still think she felt that deep down everything was Aunt Isa's fault – and left. A moment later the front door slammed.

"Aunt Isa?"

Aunt Isa picked up the kettle again and carefully poured boiling water into the teapot.

"Go with her," she said. "If she really wants to tell you what happened, then you should listen to her.

You'll be the first to know the whole truth, I believe. The rest of us have had to guess."

Star nickered at me when I opened the stable door. She probably thought I was bringing her her morning hay. I fed her a few handfuls from the floor, where she had dropped it because she likes to munch with her head over the door to her loose box. Proper breakfast would have to wait a little longer.

Mum was distractedly scratching one of the goats between its horns. It wasn't that my mum hated animals as such, she didn't... I'd been allowed to have riding lessons for a few years, before the riding school moved out of town and it became too much of a trek. Nor had she minded Cat moving in. Then again, it's difficult to keep out a cat when it can just slip through doors and walls using the wildways, but even so... Oscar's dog, Woofer, was also allowed into our flat as long as Oscar was with him.

She was scared of *wild* animals and most scared of those that could be dangerous, of course.

She turned around and checked with her Mum-vision that I was properly dressed – boots, warm jacket and a woollen hat for my damp hair. For a few seconds we stood there staring at each other, neither knowing where to start.

"When I was twelve, I made a deal with my best friend," Mum suddenly began without preamble. "Her name was Lia. Her mother was also a wildwitch, but Lia wasn't sure if she wanted to be one herself. She... she was a gentle girl, a little insecure at times, but brave in her own way. We always stuck together and so no one ever really teased us. She had brown eyes like you, but very fair hair. It was so fine and delicate and alive, her hair, it never hung straight, not even indoors, and she had to keep it out of her face with a hairband. She had a fantastic singing voice, pure and strong, the kind you just can't help listening to, and, truth be told, I think she'd rather have been a singer than a wildwitch. I was one day older than her and when our Tridecimals were coming up, we decided to help each other. First, my night, then hers. First, my task, then hers. We both felt better about doing it that way. Together we could take on anything, or so we thought."

She came to a halt and stayed silent for a while. Star snorted, and the goat Mum had been patting put its front feet on the top plank of the loose box's wall and nudged her with its head. It didn't butt her, it just nudged her. It wanted her to start scratching it again.

My mum took a deep breath.

"This is harder than I thought," she said in a low voice.

Aunt Isa had said that Mum had never told anyone the whole story.

"I saw your lynx come back," she then said. "A big cat also came to me on my Tridecimal. She came walking out from the wildways fog, a big, beautiful golden puma with eyes the colour of amber. I knew I was supposed to follow her and help her, and so that's what I did, together with Lia, just as we'd agreed. We followed the puma along the wildways to a distant mountain region, I don't know where exactly in the world. But it was desolate, rugged and hot, and the rocks were as golden as the puma, and in the sky above us there were two huge, bearded vultures circling in the updraught where the rocks made the wind rise. The mountain path was narrow and stony; you had to watch where you put your feet. The puma waited for us even though she must have thought we were terribly slow.

"We soon worked out why she needed our help. A rockfall had blocked the entrance to the puma's cave. I could see that her mammary glands were swollen and full of milk, and we could hear her cubs crying from inside the cave. Unless we could move some, if not all, of the rocks that were blocking the entrance, she wouldn't be able to get to them and they would die of hunger and thirst.

"To be honest it wasn't the most difficult challenge in the world – it needed stamina and elbow grease rather than any wildwitch skills, and that was probably just as well because even then I was nothing like Isa. But we grafted and toiled, Lia and I, digging, pushing and dragging the rocks away, even though the sun had come up and burned off the morning mists. It roasted our backs and we started feeling dizzy and thirsty because neither of us had thought to bring water or food. But we got there in the end. We managed to push aside one of the big boulders and roll it down the slope, and the cubs came tumbling out, charging at their mother. She lay down on her side and let them suckle, and by then we were so thirsty that we almost envied them.

"'Come on,' I said to Lia. 'Let's head home before one of us falls over with sunstroke. Can you find the wildways here?'

"'No,' Lia said, glancing nervously at the puma mother. 'I think we have to walk back to the place where we stepped out of the wildways fog.'

"But as we made our way down the mountain path, Lia tripped and fell. I don't know if her ankle was broken or sprained, but she couldn't put any weight on it at all. I tried carrying her, but I couldn't. I was too tired and too thirsty, I was faint from the heat and lack of water, and the path was narrow and dangerous.

"'It's no use,' Lia said. 'We'll both fall. You need to go get help, Milla. I'll wait here.'"

Mum stared into the morning darkness in the stable as if she were in a totally different place, somewhere hot, dry and desolate where the stones were bare and hard.

"I left her," she said. "I had no choice. Lia was better than me at finding her way through the wildways fog, but I went as fast as I could."

She heaved a sigh, uneven and almost rattling.

"I wasn't fast enough. I should never have left her. I should have dragged her with me, no matter how hard it was for both of us. But I didn't. And when I came back with water and food and bandages and Lia's mum... when I came back at first we couldn't find the right place. The right path. We called out and we searched everywhere, but there was no reply.

We didn't find the place until the evening. And by then Lia was gone."

Oh no. I didn't want to hear any more. Because I'd already seen it, in the glimpse of the nightmare I'd shared with my mum. The blood, the torn flesh, the sharp, white bones sticking out through the redness.

"The puma..." my mum gulped and had to start over. "The puma we'd helped... whose cubs we'd saved... do you know how it thanked us? By killing her. It ate her. There was nothing but a few bits of bone and dried blood left. She was completely helpless and wouldn't have been able to run, she couldn't even walk. It's easy to think that animals are cute, Clara, when you're here with Aunt Isa helping great tits and cute baby badgers. But the wildworld isn't like that. *Now do you understand?*"

CHAPTER TEN

Missing

Mum left. I don't know where she went; I think she just needed some fresh air. I felt the same. My Perfect Birthday had come crashing down around my ears. I'd tried mixing my ordinary world with my wildwitch world for just one day. I guess I thought that afterwards everyone would return to their usual places, Mum to her Mum-place, Dad to his Dad-place and so on, and everything would carry on as before. Only it hadn't worked out that way.

"This is a real mess," I muttered to Star as I gave her a goodbye pat on her neck. She twitched one ear politely, but she was far more interested in the hay I'd just given her.

Mum's story kept going round my mind. The puma and its cubs, the heat, the rocks, Lia... and that last incomprehensible image, flesh and dried blood, flies, bones flashing white in the fierce sun.

I did know that nature wasn't all sweetness. I'd once felt the urge to devour another living creature – it was probably the worst and most disgusting experience of my wildwitch life and, although the hunger hadn't been entirely mine, I'd come to accept that hunger and killing, predators and prey, were a part of the wildworld. I understood that a puma coming across a helplessly wounded human being might regard it as prey. But a puma that had first asked for help and received it... that it would go on to devour the person who... No. I couldn't make it add up. It was the equivalent of me using my wildwitch power to call an animal, and then killing it. I knew of only one wildwitch who'd done that, and that was Chimera. I thought that most wildwitches would rather starve than abuse their power.

When I returned to the yard, my dad was walking briskly towards the bridge.

"Where are you going?" I called out to him.

"To the car," he said. Then he stopped and came back. "Please may I borrow your phone, munchkin?" he asked. "The mechanic and the guy called Andy the Forester are on their way, and it would be good to be able to call them, if they don't turn up or they can't find the place."

"Of course."

Suddenly he looked at me more closely.

"Is something wrong?"

"No," I said. "Not really."

"If you're not comfortable lending it to me—"

"No. It's not that. It's something else. It's a bit complicated." I fished the phone out of my pocket. "Here, take it."

In a way, I really did want to tell him everything. About my own Tridecimal and Mum and the puma. About the disturbing thoughts that churned in my head. But right now it was easier just to return him to the Dad-place than to try and explain.

He could tell that something was up. But the car and the mechanic and Andy the Forester were waiting, and he was in a hurry, I could see that.

"We'll talk about it when I get back," he said. "Deal?"

I just nodded. Because we both thought that there would be loads of time to talk later. Neither of us could have known that this wasn't exactly how things turned out...

I went back inside the house and helped Aunt Isa lay the table. Oscar had finally got up – he's not exactly an early bird.

"Where's your mum?" he asked sleepily.

"Oh... outside."

"Right." He took a bite of a toasted bread roll. Then he seemed to be counting slowly as he worked out that someone else was missing from the table.

"Where's your dad?"

"He's gone to get the car."

"Right."

While we were eating, Mum came back. She didn't say very much and I don't suppose that I did either, but luckily The Nothing was chatting away nineteen to the dozen, and all the rest of us had to say was "yes" or "no" or "really" every now and then.

We were doing the dishes when a boxy red van pulled into the yard. ALF'S AUTO it said in large letters on the side, so it had to be the mechanic. Bumble barked like crazy – having a strange car to bark at was a rare treat for him.

The man who got out seemed to be in a foul mood. He slammed the car door with a bang and, before we'd had time to let him in, he was hammering his fist so hard against the door that Bumble barked even louder, and now not just for fun.

"Bumble, go to your basket," Aunt Isa said in a low, but firm voice. Bumble looked at her sceptically, but did as he was told.

"I need the car keys," said the grumpy man in the boiler suit the moment Aunt Isa opened the door.

"The car keys?" Aunt Isa said.

"Yes. For the Volvo. Is this the wrong house?"

"No, but... my brother-in-law has them. It's his car. I thought he was meeting you there?"

"Well, I wouldn't be standing here then, would I?"

"And you didn't see him on the road coming here?"

"Nope. Apart from the lumberjacks there wasn't anybody."

Aunt Isa looked at him. "I think it's best that we all drive back with you," she said.

"Listen, lady, does that look like a taxi to you?" He jerked his thumb in the direction of the van.

"No. But we won't all fit into my car and, besides, it's practically running on the rims." Aunt Isa did actually own a car, an ancient Morris Minor, but she rarely used it.

When the mechanic realized that "we" meant two grown women, a girl, a boy and a very big dog, he became even more disgruntled, but saying no to Aunt Isa once she gets an idea into her head is very difficult, even for ALF'S AUTO. Mum and Aunt Isa sat in the front with the mechanic, while Oscar, Bumble and I were allowed to go in the back.

"That's seriously illegal," Auto-Alf grumbled. "If I get fined..."

"We're not on a public road," Aunt Isa said calmly. "Start the car."

At first it was great fun to rattle along inside the murky van rather than sit on an ordinary car seat, but the excitement waned quickly.

"Ouch," Oscar said when the car bumped over a particularly stubborn tree root and a heavy toolbox skidded across the metal floor to slam into his shin. Bumble was standing stiffly with all four legs further apart than usual; he wasn't looking very excited either.

I started to wonder what could have happened to my dad.

"It's strange..." I said.

"What?"

"That he wasn't waiting by the car. After all, that's why he went."

"Maybe he'll be there when we arrive," Oscar said.

"Yes, but then why wasn't he there when the mechanic turned up?"

"Perhaps he had to do something."

"Like what? We're in the middle of a forest, Oscar. There's nothing to do."

"Pee. Maybe he needed to pee?"

"Well, all right, maybe. But how long does that take?"

"Stop worrying. We'll be there in a moment, and your dad is bound to be there."

But he wasn't. Andy the Forester and his colleague were busy cutting up the spruce and stacking the logs by the roadside. The Volvo looked pretty much the same, only it was missing its windscreen. There was no sign of my dad. Andy hadn't seen him either.

"No," he said calmly, turning over the chewing gum in his mouth. "There's no one here. Would you like the wood, Isa? After all, it fell on your road."

"Thanks, Andy. I would like that." Though Aunt Isa didn't look as if winter fuel was foremost in her mind.

"Oscar," I said. "Try calling my phone."

"Why?"

"Because Dad borrowed it."

Oscar did as I had asked.

"There's no reply," he said after a few rings. But I'd seen Bumble prick up his ears.

"Call it again," I said.

"But there's no—"

"Just do it. And then be quiet and listen."

This time I was almost certain that I could hear it too – StarPhone's little welcome jingle, which was the ringtone that it came pre-programmed with. I hadn't had time to change it yet. Bumble let out a low woof and raced past the logs and out into the tall, yellow grass, where I'd looked for deer last night, just before the tree came down.

"Follow me," I said to Oscar and ran after Bumble. "And keep ringing!"

We headed in the direction of the sound and Bumble as best we could. A few hundred metres from the car, hidden in the meadow grass, we found my new phone.

But where was Dad?

"I don't like this," Mum said to Aunt Isa in a low voice. She didn't think that I could hear what she was saying, but I could. "This reeks of your witchcraft."

"What do you mean?" Aunt Isa said coldly. "Are you accusing me of making Clara's dad disappear now?"

"No, not directly. Or rather, not you, but some of your witch friends or witch enemies."

"Milla, seriously. What makes you think this has anything to do with the wildworld?"

"In *my* world grown men don't vanish into thin air!"

They were still trying to have a conversation that couldn't be overheard, and somehow the lowered voices made the argument even more clenched and hissy.

"Please stop arguing," I said. "And yes – I can hear every word."

They both had the decency to look embarrassed.

"Clara is right," Aunt Isa said. "This isn't getting us anywhere. We have to look for him – and I hope you won't mind if some of my wildfriends help us…"

Mum swallowed something and settled for shaking her head.

"OK," she said. "What do we do?"

"How about Bumble?" I said. "Can he help us?"

"He's not much of a bloodhound, but we can always give it a try," Aunt Isa said. "After all, he did find the phone."

"Mostly because it was ringing," Oscar pointed out. "It's a shame Woofer isn't here. He's great at finding things."

Woofer was a labrador and did indeed have a great nose – especially when looking for treats. But apart from that he wasn't really an action hero kind of a dog.

"I'll call Hoot-Hoot," Aunt Isa said. "He doesn't like flying in daylight much, but he hears everything that moves."

When Hoot-Hoot appeared in the sky, however, he wasn't alone. A big flock of rooks and jackdaws were chasing him, and not even Aunt Isa could make them lay off. Hoot-Hoot landed on Aunt Isa's shoulder, and though he tried hard to look all owl-dignified and impervious, I couldn't help thinking of a little kid climbing up onto his mum's lap to stop the bigger kids teasing him. At night Hoot-Hoot was king, a silent, fearless and lethal hunter. In the daytime the other birds got their own back.

"Shoo! Go away," Aunt Isa said, flapping her hands at the most intrusive jackdaws. "Pesky birds."

They took off but landed again on the nearest trees, where they waited to pounce. It was clear that we couldn't expect any aerial assistance from Hoot-Hoot today.

"Please would you hold him?" Aunt Isa asked and persuaded Hoot-Hoot to hop from her shoulder onto mine. "I have to try something else."

She sat down in the tall grass and closed her eyes.

"Be careful," Mum said, and for once sounded as if she was a little worried for her sister.

Aunt Isa smiled and didn't mention that Journeying – wildwitch style mind-travel – for her was about as everyday an occurrence as a trip to the shops was for Mum.

"I will," was all she said. It was true that Journeying could be dangerous if you didn't know what you were doing. Martin from my school – I tried very hard not to call him Martin the Meanie even in my thoughts – had been badly hurt because I hadn't been in control of my own involuntary Journeyings. But Aunt Isa was a zillion times better at it than me.

When you went Journeying, you borrowed an animal's eyes, ears and nose. It felt as if you suddenly *were* the animal, and it could be very confusing to have wings instead of arms, for example, and a strong urge to eat raw mice. Right now Aunt Isa was looking for a suitable bird – maybe one of the cheeky rooks. A bird flying very high above us, one that could see much more than we could down here on earth.

Hoot-Hoot made a low, clicking sound with his beak. I don't think he liked Aunt Isa leaving us like this, but he stayed perched on my shoulder, holding on just tight enough to keep his balance. Given what a big bird he was, he wasn't nearly as heavy as you would think, but you could certainly feel he was there.

"What do you think happened to Dad?" I said quietly to Mum.

"I don't know, Clara Mouse." I suddenly realized that Mum had been more nervous than me all along. I wasn't used to worrying about my dad, if anything it was the other way around, and that's how it's supposed to be, isn't it? Besides, my dad never did anything weird or dangerous. He was just Dad. He went to work, he went on holidays with me or to the cinema, and even when we crashed into trees and stuff, he was calm and normal and unruffled. The reason I got scared now was mostly because I could feel that Mum was scared – only I didn't know why.

Then it dawned on me. She was thinking about the lynx. The lynx with the golden eyes and the long claws.

"It didn't do it," I blurted out.

"What do you mean?" she asked.

"You think the lynx... took him. But it hasn't!"

"You know nothing about that," Mum said. "You've got no idea what's happened."

"Neither do you!"

Oscar was staring at us, his mouth half open. If he said one word about how "super-cool" it would be to be attacked by a lynx, I would thump him. But he didn't.

Aunt Isa sighed and stirred as if to check she had human arms and legs again.

"I'm not quite sure," she said. "But I think we should try heading in that direction." She pointed across the meadow towards the edge of the forest.

When we started walking, we heard a yell of protest behind us.

"Oi!" Auto-Alf called out from up the road. "What about those car keys?"

"They're not here," Mum snapped back. "Not right now."

"Do you want that car fixed or not? Whatever you decide, I'll charge you mileage. And an hourly rate for all the time I've wasted."

"Just send us your bill," Mum snarled.

Auto-Alf straightened up and was actually shaking his fist in the air. I had never seen anyone do that in real life.

"Stupid cow! Don't bother calling me another time."

Then he got back in his boxy van and drove past the Volvo so closely that the wing mirror snapped back with a loud bang, and he disappeared down the road at a speed that most definitely wouldn't do his van any good. Then again, he could always repair it himself.

"He called your mum a stupid cow!" Oscar was outraged. "He's the one who's stupid. Why bother turning up if he's in such a bad mood? He could always have said no."

"I guess he wanted the money," I said absentmindedly. Auto-Alf and his tantrums weren't exactly at the top of my list right now. Because what if Mum was right? What if the lynx, like the puma, had ended up attacking a human being who was only trying to help? How was it to know that it was *my* dad?

"Lynxes are shy," Aunt Isa said, more to my mum than to me, but it felt as if she could read my mind. "They stay away from people, they don't attack them."

"Let's hope so," my mum said grimly.

We started walking through the tall, yellow grass, not in single file, but spread out in a fan, so that we covered a greater area of the meadow. We called out and we searched. I wasn't wearing my watch, so I don't know for how long.

When we'd almost reached the edge of the forest on the far side of the meadow, something low, heavy and awkward came flapping in a jumpy, uneven line across the grass. It was The Nothing. I wouldn't have thought she could fly this far, but here she was, panting and groaning; I could hear her gasping and struggling before she landed a short distance from us with all the elegance of a wet dishcloth dropping onto the floor.

"I... I... I've seen..." She was so out of breath that she could barely force out the words: "... seen him!"

"My dad?" I said.

"Clara's... dad," she wheezed. "Yes."

"Where?"

"There," she said, pointing with the tip of her wing. "He... he's lying very still, and he doesn't... he doesn't say anything..."

Bending down so quickly that Hoot-Hoot flapped his wings in protest and flew back to Aunt Isa, I picked up The Nothing, small, wet and exhausted as she was, and started to run.

CHAPTER ELEVEN

The Leech

He was lying at the edge of the wood, right where the meadow became a forest again. New ferns had started shooting up through the soil, but the old, brown, withered ones made it difficult to spot him.

I reached him first; Oscar normally ran faster than me, but he didn't have The Nothing helping him by pointing and calling out: "That way. No, more to the right!" And: "Right there! Can't you see him?"

He was lying flat on his back as though he was just passing the time by gazing at the clouds. But his eyes were closed and, for one horrible moment, I was afraid that he might be dead. Then I saw that he was breathing – his nostrils flared, his chest slowly heaved and sank.

"Dad?" I whispered.

He didn't reply, of course. If he hadn't heard us scream and shout for the last half hour, it would take more than a whisper to wake him. I squatted down on my haunches and carefully touched his cheek.

My fingers were cold, but he was even colder. What was wrong with him?

"Is it my fault?" The Nothing asked.

"Your fault? No, why would it be?"

"Because... he wasn't supposed to see me, and then I got myself seen anyway. And I could tell that he went all wrong when he spotted me. All wrong. Perhaps it made him ill?"

"No one gets ill just from looking at you," I said. "It's not your fault. Quite the opposite. After all, you were the one who found him."

"Yes," The Nothing said, looking much happier. "I did! All by myself!"

"How did you know that we were looking for him?"

"When Hoot-Hoot flew off. He went to look for something, I could feel it. And then I thought perhaps I could help. Though I'm not very good at flying." She moved her limbs gingerly. "My wings are really sore now..."

I knew I was supposed to say nice things and keep praising her, but all I could think about right now was my dad. I unbuttoned the top of his shirt to make sure that he could breathe.

And there it was. Right where his neck joins his body. A big, fat, black-and-brown leech.

I tore it off on impulse. Only afterwards did I remember that you were supposed to make them let go. I just wanted it *off* him, so I pulled hard. Perhaps that was why there was so much blood everywhere. His shirt and his jacket were soaked, and the brown ferns were dyed red.

"What's happened?" said Oscar, who had been close behind me most of the way. "Did he get stabbed or something?"

"No..." I flung away the leech and pressed both hands against the wound as if trying to force all the blood back into my dad.

He stirred and half opened his eyes. His gaze was strangely veiled as if he weren't quite present.

"Clara," he mumbled. "Colours. Colours everywhere. Why is everything turning red?"

Then his eyelids closed, and although I called him and shook him gently, he didn't come round again.

"Let me have a look," Aunt Isa said, dropping to her knees next to me. "Where has all that blood come from?"

"A leech," I said. "There was a leech and I... pulled it off." It was my fault, I thought. "Should I have left it alone?"

"Possibly," Aunt Isa said. "Depends what kind it was. Where is it?"

"I... I just threw it away."

Aunt Isa placed her hands where mine had just been. She started singing, a slow and heavy wildsong that made it hard to breathe. But the blood stopped flowing and that was more important.

"You said... you said it wasn't dangerous," I stuttered. "When Kahla was bitten."

"And it isn't, normally," she said. "He'll wake up soon, you'll see. Maybe he fell and hit his head and that explains why... A cup of willow bark tea and a bit of wildsong, and he'll be right as rain. Don't be scared, Clara, we'll get him well again. One doesn't die from being bitten by a leech. You go get Star, so we can bring your dad home."

"There's no way he's going back to yours," Mum said, ashen-faced but very determined. "He's going to a hospital. No more witchcraft! Clara, give me your phone."

People don't die from being bitten by a leech. Aunt Isa had said so, so it must be true. I gave my Mum the phone.

"I'm perfectly capable—" my aunt began. But Mum cut her off.

"No. Ambulance. Doctor. Hospital. And I don't want him full of all sorts of herbal hocus pocus when he's admitted."

T he ambulance rattled slowly across the meadow and up onto the road. It had arrived with flashing lights and a siren, but it drove off quietly, which I took to mean that whatever was wrong with my dad wasn't serious and urgent.

Mum had gone with him in the ambulance.

She'd looked at me with a weird, frozen expression.

"Stay here," was all she'd said. "I'll call."

Then the doors were closed and the ambulance set off.

Aunt Isa put her hand on my shoulder.

"It's all right," she said. "He'll get well again. With or without herbal hocus pocus..."

I nodded.

"But, Aunt Isa..."

"Yes."

"You don't pass out just because you're bitten by a leech... or two, for that matter." Because on my dad's chest and arms there had been big, round plunger-like marks, just like the ones on Kahla's leg. He had been bitten at least five times, so perhaps it had been more than one leech.

"No," Aunt Isa said. "Most of the time you don't even notice. Leeches produce a substance that numbs the skin. And besides..." she looked around pensively, "besides, there shouldn't be leeches here at all. They live in ponds and lakes and wetlands, and this meadow just isn't wet enough."

"Maybe he walked through a wet place?"

"Maybe."

But I could tell from looking at her that that wasn't the whole story. There had to be more to it. The question was what.

"Maybe Kahla did get bitten near your house, rather than at home," I ventured.

"It's beginning to look like it."

She closed her eyes like she had when she went Journeying to find Dad, but this time it was in order to use her wildsense better. It was one of the first skills she'd taught me.

"What are you looking for?" I asked.

"I really want to find that leech again," she mumbled without opening her eyes.

OK, I thought. You can do this too. Aunt Isa doesn't have to do everything for you.

I closed my eyes. Then I covered my ears with my hands. It was best to shut out the other senses as much as possible, and I needed all the help I could get.

The place was teeming with life. In the earth, under the leaves, in the treetops, in the sky, among the ferns. I could sense Oscar right next to me in a strange, intimate way. He and I have a blood bond, almost like Cat and me. It might just have been a silly game we'd made up – all right, one that Oscar had made up – one afternoon when we were bored and he thought we needed a little excitement. But silly or not, we'd done it. A bit of his blood had mingled with a bit of mine. In the wildworld such things mattered.

But I wasn't looking for Oscar right now. And how the heck do you find one tiny, sorry spark of life in a noisy choir of living things?

Blood. It was about blood.

My dad's blood was in the leech, and I was my father's daughter. I could follow that trail, it was like a delicate, red path, a thread of life and blood as thin as a cobweb. Got it!

I opened my eyes. Took three steps to the right, rummaged around the ferns and there it was. The hardest part was to pick it up again. Gross doesn't even begin to describe it.

"Here it is," I said, holding it up to Aunt Isa.

She opened her eyes.

"You found it!" she said. "Well done, wildwitch..."

I could see that she was both delighted and surprised. She wasn't used to me trying things out or learning new skills without first being encouraged. I have to admit that I rarely did something with wildwitchcraft unless I had no choice. Or that was how I used to be – before my Tridecimal...

Aunt Isa stuck her hand in her pocket and found one of the linen bags she uses when gathering herbs. She always carried a few around because, as she would say, you never knew what you'd find. The best stuff often turned up when you weren't even looking. She turned the bag inside out and used it as a kind of glove before taking the leech from me.

"Hmmm," she said. "This is no ordinary leech. I need to go home and look it up." She pulled the bag over the leech and tightened the strings at the opening so it couldn't escape.

While we waited for news from the hospital, Aunt Isa kept us busy studying the leech. I wasn't sure whether it was really because she thought it was important or just a diversion so I wouldn't think too much about my dad, but she put the creature in the middle of the kitchen table in a jam jar filled with water. The Nothing helped us find everything the house had by way of leech reference books, and we sat down with one each and started flicking through them, Oscar, The Nothing, Aunt Isa and me.

The leech was still alive despite the trip in the fabric bag. It sucked onto the glass with one end and probed around with its other like an amputated, wriggling finger. It was also about the size of a finger and most of its body was dark brown apart from a vivid yellow stripe down one side. If I looked carefully, I could see that its body was built around a skeleton of rings like those slinkies that can walk down stairs.

"Is this it?" Oscar asked, showing us a picture of a brown leech with a stripe along its side. We looked at his book and then at our leech.

"No," Aunt Isa said. "That's not it. It's similar, but ours has a broader stripe and more rings than that one."

So we carried on looking.

At long last Mum called. Her voice came across with perfect clarity on my StarPhone.

"He's going to be all right," she said. "He's a little confused, and can't quite remember what happened, and he's very tired. They think he's lost a lot of blood, but that he'll be fine as long as he rests and drinks plenty of fluids."

Lost a lot of blood... I remembered the bloodbath I'd caused and felt a stab of guilt.

"When will he be allowed home?" I asked.

"We'll stay here tonight. The hospital has accommodation where we can both stay, so that he can be examined and hopefully discharged tomorrow."

"OK."

"Clara Mouse, I'm sorry if I sounded a bit harsh."

"It's OK."

She'd been scared and worried. But then again, so had I.

"I know that you're having a nice time with Aunt Isa," she said. "But please don't..."

"Don't what?"

"No, forget it. You've already told me not to interfere in your wildwitch life." She was hurt, I could hear it. And I felt really bad inside when Mum got upset. But *some* things I had to decide for myself, and this was one of them.

"It's the way it has to be, Mum."

"No," she said. "*You've* decided it's the way it has to be. And I just have to learn to live with it."

She hung up. I sat for a while with the phone in my hand before I stuffed it into my pocket.

"How is he?" Oscar wanted to know.

"Better. They're keeping him overnight." Then I remembered that Oscar's mum was waiting for him to come home. We'd called her last night and explained about the tree and promised to be back later today, but that was before a leech upset our plans. "Oscar, what about you? Shouldn't we take you back? If we go on the wildways...?"

"I think that's going to be difficult to explain," he said. "It would be better to call and say why we're delayed and that I'll come back tomorrow."

I handed him my StarPhone without another word, and he went into the living room to call his mum.

"Aunt Isa?"

"Yes?"

"Why is it so important that we find out what kind of leech it is?"

"Because I'm fairly sure it doesn't belong here," my aunt said. "And if it doesn't – then someone or something brought it here."

Oscar came back while I was still mulling over her words.

"It's OK," he said, "I'm allowed to stay until tomorrow."

"Was she angry?" I asked.

He pulled a face. "She prefers it when people keep their promises."

"I imagine most lawyers are like that," Aunt Isa said with a wry smile. "And we can take you back, it's no problem."

"No. She did say it was OK. Deep down I think it suits her because she has an important meeting tomorrow she needs to prepare for. And being here is *definitely* more fun..."

"And what if we're not here?" Aunt Isa said.

"Er... what do you mean?"

"I was thinking... there's a wildwitch who knows just about everything there is to know about leeches.

And she lives quite close to Raven Kettle. Two birds with one stone, perhaps."

Because of Dad getting ill, I'd almost forgotten that we'd agreed to talk to the Raven Mothers about my Tridecimal.

"You mean I get to meet the Raven Mothers? And a leech witch?" Oscar's freckled face lit up in a wide grin. "Super-cool!"

CHAPTER TWELVE

The House of the Leech Witch

"Thousands of animals..." Thuja said. "I've never heard of that before..."

She'd invited us into her sitting room, one of the many cave-like rooms and guest quarters dug into the circular crater wall of Raven Kettle. It was a bit dark because there was only one window in the whole of her house, but that didn't matter to Thuja. She had been born completely blind...

When I first met her, I'd never have guessed. Thuja had led the circle of Raven Mothers and I knew her better than the others because she'd looked after us the first time I visited Raven Kettle. Back then she'd moved just like a seeing person, no fumbling, no hesitation. But only because she had borrowed the eyes of her raven.

That raven was dead now, killed by Chimera, like most of the Raven Mothers' other birds. For the first time in her adult life, Thuja was blind again, and it would take time before a raven chick from this spring's new brood had grown big enough to assist her. Thuja could see by using other animals as hosts, but what she got to see was entirely random – and not much use if you were looking for the teapot, say.

So now Thuja had a boy who helped her out. Arkus was short and skinny with dark hair, and he was terribly shy. He hardly dared look at us, especially not at Aunt Isa. But he made us tea and ran off to fetch buns from Raven Kettle's own bakery.

"Arkus is a kind of foundling," Thuja explained. "He was taken from his mum and put into a home because he made the mistake of telling people he could talk to animals. But he ran away from what was by all accounts a pretty awful place and made his own way here by asking the birds. He is a very gifted boy. He reads aloud to me, fluently, even though he's only eight years old and hasn't had the easiest time at school."

"What about his mum?" Aunt Isa wanted to know. "Does she know where he is?"

"Yes. We found her. She visits him as often as she can, but she says he's better off here, and I think she's right. Here he can learn everything he needs to, and no one calls him psychotic because he understands what the birds are saying. If we could, we would persuade his mum to move out here too, but she says she's not ready, not yet."

Three of the sitting-room walls were lined from floor to ceiling with sagging bookshelves, enough to keep Arkus busy reading aloud for years. I tried imagining what it must have been like to be called crazy and put in some kind of institution because you happened to have been born with wildwitch powers. Perhaps I was lucky that my mum knew that wildwitches were real, even though she wanted nothing to do with them.

"Clara?" Thuja said.

"Yes?"

"Please may I touch your forehead?"

I'd tried this several times before so I knew why she was asking. I stood still in front of her while she rested her fingertips gently on my forehead and started humming a faint wildsong. This would allow her to see fragments of what had happened on my Tridecimal.

"Remarkable," she said. "So many animals at once... how can they all need your help?"

"That's exactly what we want to know," Aunt Isa said. "I've never heard of a young wildwitch given so... complex a task."

"Vitus Bluethroat was told to help a swarm of bees," Thuja said. "In theory, he had more animals to deal with than Clara, but they all wanted the same thing. Clara, did you have any sense of *what* they wanted you to do?"

I pondered her question.

"They wanted me to say yes," I then answered. "But I still don't know what I've said yes to."

"Did any animals stand out?"

"I think so because a few of them came closer to me than the others. An otter. A lynx. A bison – and a mouse."

Thuja smiled. "Those are very different animals."

"Yes."

"Two predators, two herbivores. The smallest one was very small, and the biggest also very big. What could they have in common?"

"I don't know."

"Me neither. I want to help, but..." she sighed and looked a little frustrated. "You're a very unusual wildwitch, Clara Ash. And you have a habit of getting mixed up in very unusual problems."

Somehow it didn't sound like praise.

"Sorry," I mumbled.

"What for? You are what you are. And it's not your fault that thousands of animals decided to ask for your help at once."

We said goodbye to Thuja, and set off for the house of the leech witch. "Quite close" turned out to be about half an hour's walk through the forest that surrounded Raven Kettle. A few black birds circled above us, but it was nothing compared to the host of ravens, crows and rooks that used to live at Raven Kettle. Their absence made me sad.

"There's just something missing, isn't there?" I said to Aunt Isa.

"Yes," my aunt said. "So much has been lost. And I don't know if we'll ever get it back."

Would Thuja have been able to help us more if she'd still had her raven? I didn't know. Raven Kettle had been a place where every wildwitch could go to seek justice, a place where you could get help and advice when serious dangers threatened the wild-world. It was not like that at the moment.

"Thuja isn't the only one who's blind now," I said.

Aunt Isa heaved a sigh. "No, sadly. Now we all are."

The path was becoming wetter and more boggy, and I realized that a wildwitch interested in leeches would probably want to live near them. I was glad I was wearing boots and trousers. This wasn't a place where you'd want to run around in shorts...

The soil was black and had an acidic, sour smell. Lurid green moss grew densely on tree trunks and fallen branches, and I could see puddles of shiny water between tufts and tussocks of tall grass. Once it was proper summer there would probably be flowers and leaves and light, but right now the colours were mostly black, brown and moss green. In some places mats of woven reeds had been put down to create at least some semblance of firm ground, but I could still hear an ominous slurping as I walked.

"There it is," Oscar said, in among the trees. "Wow, that's super-cool! It's on stilts!"

I don't know what I'd been expecting, but certainly not this: the house was painted in glossy pastel colours, primrose yellow, mint green and frosty pink; it looked more like icing on a cake than house paint. Among all the brown and black it stood out like a flashing set of traffic lights, and what with all the "icing", I couldn't help thinking of gingerbread houses and the sort of witch supposed to live in them... It sat in the middle of a small green island and was indeed raised a metre above the ground on fat red posts. Perhaps the island flooded sometimes? A small red bridge led across the black water and, though a gate blocked one end of the bridge, a sign read "Welcome! The door is open!" in letters so big I wondered what the point of the gate was.

There was a bell on a chain next to the gate; Aunt Isa rang it a couple of times.

"Enter!" A deep, not very feminine voice called out to us through one of the gingerbread house's open windows. "Can't you read?"

Aunt Isa raised an eyebrow, but she said nothing.

"She's not very polite, is she?" Oscar whispered.

"Shh!" I hissed.

Aunt Isa opened the gate and we walked up the garden path to the pink door. We didn't knock, we just went right in. Following the surly reaction to Aunt Isa's ringing the bell, we thought we might as well.

The house was just as colourful on the inside. The floor was sky blue and the planks that made up the wooden walls were painted in stripes of white, pink or pale yellow, keeping up the frosted look. There was white wicker furniture boosted with plump, shiny silk cushions in flowery, checked or dotted patterns, and a cluster of coloured glass tea-light lanterns hung from the ceiling. On the walls were pictures of puppies and kittens in completely unrealistic colours, and on a shelf between two candles was a heart-shaped silver picture frame holding a photograph of a little girl with blonde pigtails, huge pink bows and big, somewhat shy, brown eyes. There wasn't a single leech in sight, but next to one of the two coffee tables in the living room there was a... eh, well...

A frogman,was the word that sprang to mind. He didn't have a single hair on his head, his eyes stood out so much they didn't look quite human, and his mouth was a wide lipless gash that took up the whole of his lower face. His skin was glossy and smooth, almost the colour of pickled green olives, apart from a few brown spots spreading like big freckles up his neck and across his bald pate. If a princess had tried kissing this frog, she must have given up too soon, because there was still a long way to go before he could be described as a prince. His neat black suit and worn grey bow tie discreetly contrasted with the explosion of colour around him, and I had the distinct impression that he hadn't been in charge of the décor.

It soon became clear why he was crotchety. He was sitting in an old-fashioned wicker wheelchair with a tall back, and his legs were covered by a grey-and-white checked rug. He clearly couldn't just jump up and open doors and garden gates for random visitors.

"What do you want?" he demanded. "Alichia isn't here."

His eyes were the most attractive feature about him, I thought. Golden-brown and strangely warm in the middle of his sour and unapproachable face.

"Oh, what a shame," Aunt Isa said. "We've brought her a leech that we hoped she could identify. We've never seen its kind before. My name is Isa Ash, and this is my niece, Clara and her friend Oscar."

"Aha," he said, then added reluctantly, "My name is Fredric. I'm Alichia's lodger."

"Do you know when she'll be back?" I asked.

"No idea; whenever it suits the lady to turn up," he said. "She's been gone for days now, and I haven't had so much as a message or an apology."

A half-finished game of patience was lying on the table in front of him. Probably neither his first nor his last; the playing cards looked worn and dog-eared.

"Have you lived here long?" Oscar asked.

Fredric scowled at him. "And how is that any of your business, young man?"

"Er... I don't suppose it is. I was just asking."

The wide mouth was a long, flat line without a hint of a smile.

"For ever. Ad infinitum. Ad nauseam. That means until it makes you sick, young man. I'd throw up if I could."

Aunt Isa studied him for a little while.

"Excuse me," she said. "But I can see that you're unwell. Would you mind if I tried helping you?"

He looked up at her angrily. "I'm not some injured little animal for you to fuss over, lady."

"No. But seeing as you're Alichia's lodger, you probably know that wildwitches can help people sometimes."

"That's exactly what Madam Alichia claimed and the reason I've paid a small fortune to live in this vulgar confection of a house. But so far there has been little improvement. And the side-effects are bizarre. Well, if there's nothing else, then..." He pointed to his game of patience. "I was in the middle of something."

"Do you know where she is?"

"I'm not her private secretary." He made a point of turning over a card from the pile, peering at it and putting it into another pile. As far as I could see, the chances of his game coming out were small.

"Well, then we're sorry for disturbing you."

We'd almost left when he decided to be helpful after all.

"Westmark," he said. "She thinks I don't know, but I saw her peer at the wildways maps. That woman is the least discreet creature I've ever met..." He aimed a long, greenish forefinger at a pile of papers on the second table. I couldn't help sneaking a peek, though really that was just another form of snooping. And quite right. At the top of the pile was a map of some of the wildways, and there was a big circle around the name Westmark. Shanaia's home. What was the leech witch doing there, I wondered? And might that explain why Shanaia had failed to turn up for my birthday?

CHAPTER THIRTEEN

Thunder and Lightning

I tried calling my mum, but the call went straight to voicemail.

"You've reached Milla Ash, freelance journalist. I'm afraid I can't take your call right now..."

What was the point of having the world's coolest mobile if Mum's was turned off? Then I remembered that most hospitals have rules about phones, so maybe she'd had to switch it off. I decided to text her instead, but couldn't think of anything other than: "How are things going?" It didn't even come close to voicing all the questions I had: how was my dad doing, had he come round again, could he remember more about what happened, why had he ended up so far from the car, and how had he been bitten by at least one unpleasant leech of a sort that not even Aunt Isa knew about? Plus about a million other things. I heaved a sigh, then I sent my stupid little text message. It was better than nothing, and at least she'd know that I was thinking about her and Dad.

"Now what?" I asked.

"We're going to Westmark, of course," Oscar said in a way that implied you had to be seriously dense to even ask. "Two birds with one stone again! We'll find this leech lady of yours *and* Shanaia can tell us why she didn't show up yesterday."

I suddenly wasn't sure that I wanted to kill even one bird, let alone two. It seemed quite a cruel thing to do, once you stopped to think about it. A bit like "more than one way to skin a cat". It reminded me too much of Chimera. And anyway, we hadn't exactly hit the target with our stones so far.

"Does that mean we have to walk all the way back to Raven Kettle?" I said.

"I wonder if I can find a wildway a little nearer to where we are," Aunt Isa said, "if you're sure that's where we're going."

"I guess so," I said. "Oscar is right; if we don't, this has all been a complete waste of time."

The sky over Westmark was low, heavy and dark not only because it was now evening, but far more so because storm clouds the colour of tarmac had gathered over the sea and were blocking out the sun. Four storm petrels were skipping about in the updraught over the cliff, small dark shapes flitting among the herring gulls like foolhardy sparrows taunting a hawk...

Seeing them this close to the shore did not bode well for the weather.

"There's a storm brewing," I said. "Do you think there'll be thunder?"

I'd barely said the words when a distant rumble rolled towards us.

"Wouldn't surprise me," Aunt Isa said with a small smile. "Come on; let's get inside where it's dry."

It had already started to rain: big, wet drops that turned into coin-sized spots when they hit the fabric of my coat.

Westmark was built on top of an old ruin, and its crumbling castle wall was now only a garden wall, but much thicker. The cast-iron gate squeaked on rusty hinges when Aunt Isa pushed it open and, at the same moment, an even sharper cry rang out above us.

"Kiiiiiihr!" It was Kitti, Shanaia's kestrel, swooping down on us like a fighter plane – it felt a bit menacing when she did that, but I think it was her way of saying hello.

The door was opened, but not by Shanaia. Instead, a much chubbier woman appeared on the doorstep. Her hair was partly covered by a flowered scarf and her candy-striped, flouncy skirt flapped in the wind like a signal flag, powder blue, mint and pink, so I was fairly sure she must be Alichia. She certainly wore the same cake frosting colours as her house.

"Come inside, come inside," she urged us, "before the storm breaks!"

We hurried up. When I got nearer, I could see that the hair sticking out from under her scarf was the colour of honey, and her smiley eyes looked like two raisins in her round and friendly face.

"Isa!" she said and she sounded excited. "I don't know if you remember me, but I remember you. It's Alichia – don't you recognize me?"

"Of course," my aunt said. "How nice to see you again."

"And *you* must be Clara!" Alichia continued in a tone of voice that made it clear how absolutely brilliant it was to finally meet me.

I returned her smile – it was hard not to.

"But who are you? I don't know you." The latter was addressed to Oscar.

"This is my friend Oscar," I said. "He came to my birthday party. Only so many things happened that we haven't got round to... returning him home yet." I made it sound as if he were a pair of old PE shoes left behind at school. But there was something about Alichia that made you tell her more than you'd intended, and so I blurted the words out rather clumsily.

"Oh, that's right, your birthday. Congratulations, darling. A Tridecimal is a big day! Shanaia was *so* sorry to miss it, but she isn't feeling all that well, poor little lamb."

"Er... thank you. What's wrong with her?" It felt a bit weird to be chatting to a total stranger who called me darling as if we had known each other for ever, but then again... she was really nice. She meant well. She seemed so friendly and warm that I struggled to understand how she put up with miserable old Fredric in her house.

"Well, you see, that's why I'm here. She was bitten by a leech."

A leech. Just like Kahla and my dad? What was it with those leeches?

KA-booooooooooooooooooooooommmmmmmm mmmmmm...

A crack of thunder broke right above our heads and shivered the window panes and the walls themselves; a flash of lightning followed the very next second. The light was so bright I had to close my eyes for a moment.

"Now *do* come inside," Alichia said again. "What are we doing standing out here chatting, when the sky is about to open..."

It was as if the flash of lightning had split the clouds. One minute the rain had been a spattering of big but singular drops. The next it was like standing under a shower turned to maximum.

The three of us hurried through the door and Alichia slammed it hard behind us to shut out the storm. Even so, those few seconds were enough for my hair to be soaked through and cling to my face, and I could feel little streams of rain trickle down my neck and under my collar.

"A leech," Aunt Isa said sharply. "What kind?"

"Well, that's the funny thing," Alichia said. "I thought I knew every leech in the wildworld, but I've never seen one of these before."

Rainwater wasn't the only thing sending a prickly cold sensation down my spine... Aunt Isa had produced the jam jar and its inhabitant from her rucksack, but she barely had time to ask: "Do you know what this is?"

Alichia studied our fat, striped leech for barely a second.

"Yes," she said as her eyes widened in wonder. "Wherever did you get that?"

Alichia ushered us into Westmark's huge, old-fashioned kitchen, while she boiled water for tea and fetched some old towels that were clean and dry, yet somehow managed to smell a bit mouldy.

"You could easily catch a cold or worse," she said, taking out bread from the bread bin and jam from the larder with familiar ease. "How about some soup as well? You'd like a little soup, wouldn't you?"

"If it's not too much trouble..." Aunt Isa said. "But I'd like to just see Shanaia first."

"She's asleep, poor little lamb. It's best not to wake her; she'll come downstairs when she wakes up. And the soup is ready, I made it for Shanaia, and I think it's still hot." She lifted the lid of a giant pot that contained enough soup to feed an army. "So, sit yourselves down and put your feet up... I'm just sorting out some dinner for the bird." She held up a bowl full of bloody meat scraps – for Kitti probably. Then she disappeared out of the door, and I presumed she was going to Shanaia's room. I couldn't imagine Kitti being anywhere else right now, not if Shanaia was ill.

The soup was rich and red and packed with vegetables, and it warmed us up after our soaking. The thunder rumbled on outside, and the lamps in the old house flickered with every thunderclap.

"This is like something out of a horror movie," Oscar said. "Any minute now a zombie will push against the window, trying to come in and eat our brains..."

"Stop it," I said. "Zombies aren't real. Are they, Aunt Isa?"

Aunt Isa tucked a wet lock of hair behind her ear. "It depends on what you mean by zombies," she said in a calm and factual tone, as if we were just discussing some kind of exotic animal.

Why didn't she just say no outright? It would have been so much more reassuring. Oscar looked up with an excited, freckly grin, of course he did, and started questioning the expert.

"Half-rotten cadavers crawling out of their graves to eat the living," he said. "That kind of zombies. Are they real?"

"I've never heard of anything like that," Aunt Isa said. "Zombies tend to be fairly peaceful – poor, confused souls so affected by poison and witchcraft that they no longer know if they're dead or alive. You have to feel sorry for them. No, it's the person who creates the zombies you should be afraid of." She blew on her spoonful of soup to cool it down. "This business about eating the living – that sounds more like a revenant."

And that's when I got goosebumps for real because I knew only too well what a revenant was. A hurt and lonely girl called Kimmie had turned into Chimera because of a revenant.

"Someone trying to get back to life," I whispered. Someone who stole lives in order to become alive enough to "crawl out of the grave", as Oscar put it. Chimera was dead now and Kimmie's soul was free – but what had happened to the hungry one who wanted to live again?

KA-BOOOOOOOoooooooom. Yet another crash of thunder shook the house and the light disappeared for a few seconds before it came back on, flickering as if it didn't know whether it was welcome or not.

"I think we'd better light some candles," Aunt Isa said. "It looks like the power could go any minute."

Oscar leaned towards me and whispered in a distorted zombie voice.

"Brrrrraaaaiiiiinnnnnsssss. I want brrrrraaaaiiiii-nnnnnsssss..."

"Oh, stop it!"

Alichia returned and put the bowl with the meat scraps to soak in the sink – or rather, the empty bowl: Kitti had cleaned her plate.

"What dreadful weather," she said. "If it doesn't stop soon, you'd better stay the night. Then you can talk to Shanaia tomorrow morning."

"Is she still asleep?" I asked.

"Yes, indeed she is. It's probably my fault. I gave her a little of my universal mixture, and it's great for getting a good night's sleep..." She pointed to the jam jar with the leech still on the kitchen table. "Have you fed it?"

"No," Aunt Isa said dryly. "None of us really felt the urge."

"It's just another wildworld creature," Alichia said, sounding reproachful. "And a useful and interesting creature at that!"

She unscrewed the lid and retrieved the leech with practised ease. She set it down on her forearm without hesitation, where it attached itself immediately and started drawing blood.

"That's so cool," Oscar said. "Doesn't it hurt?"

"Not at all. On the contrary." Her smile was aimed at both Oscar and the hungry leech, I thought. "It numbs me first. A leech is a tiny, living pharmacy. Not only can it take away pain, it can also make the blood run without coagulating. It has been a medicinal remedy for thousands of years across the world, and it's still being used today – even by some of those stuck-up doctors who don't normally give two hoots for nature. There, my little friend. That's enough. You let go now..." She stroked the leech a couple of times with a delicate forefinger and hummed to it, and the animal released its hold as if it had been trained to do so. Alichia eased it back into the jam jar. There was a little blood on Alichia's arm, but again she hummed a couple of lengthy notes and stroked her skin, and the flow stopped. It was nothing like the bloodbath I'd caused when I tore that same leech off my dad.

"It's clearly related to the medicinal leech," she said.

"But if they're so... so good for us..." I said, "then why did Shanaia get ill? And aren't you scared of getting ill too?"

She looked a little surprised, as if the thought had never even crossed her mind.

"Of course a leech bite can get infected, just like any other wound," she said, "and they *can* transmit diseases if they've sucked blood from people or animals who were sick, but that rarely happens. I'm as fit as a butcher's dog, darling, and I'm never ill. Don't you worry about me."

I thought about my dad, who'd been lying in the grass unconscious, and who was still too out of it to remember what had happened.

"Can it make you pass out?" I asked.

"No, darling. That takes more than a single, little leech bite."

"But what if you got several? Four or five, say?"

She shook her head. "I still don't think so. Would you like to try for yourself? It's fairly sated now, so it'll only take a few drops."

She stuck her hand into the jar and fished out the leech again, but I withdrew instinctively. Quite a long way back...

"Eh... no thanks. I don't really feel like it."

"No? Are you sure? It's a useful thing for a wild-witch to know."

"I'm game!" Oscar said, sticking out his arm. "I've never tried this before!"

Neither had I, but I still wasn't tempted. I'd never been bitten by a spider or a snake either, yet that didn't make me want to "try" it! Oscar made it sound like a new rollercoaster ride.

Alichia looked at Oscar's outstretched arm, a little taken aback.

"Very well, my friend. Let's see if it wants to."

"No, Oscar, don't you dare!"

"It's completely safe," Alichia said.

"It might well be," I said. "But how are you going to explain the marks to your mum when you get home?"

Oscar quickly pulled back his arm.

"Oh, I'd forgotten about that..." he said.

An angry flash of lightning turned everything in the kitchen black and white like an old photograph. The thunder crash came rolling almost at once, and this time the lights flickered for longer.

"You drink your tea," Alichia said. "And I'll get you some bedding. You won't be going anywhere tonight."

Aunt Isa looked as if she were about to say something – perhaps she felt it was a decision we should make ourselves. But before she had time to object, there was another flash of lightning. The thunder followed instantly this time, and when the light went out, it didn't come back on.

"Looks like we'd better find some candles," Aunt Isa said.

Alichia had made up a bed for me in one of the turret rooms, that is, if you could call Westmark's rounded corner protuberances turrets – they weren't really *tall* enough. The raindrops pelted the window-pane, the storm raged and the trees creaked. I won't get a wink of sleep, I thought. I was dog-tired and was desperate for a good night's rest, but there was something about the thunder... maybe I'd paid too much attention to Oscar's ridiculous zombie stories. I certainly jumped every time there was a flash of lightning and the shadows in the room turned pitch-black and scary.

There was a click and the door opened – softly and carefully – as if whoever was outside didn't want to be seen or heard.

"Who is it?" I said, possibly a little louder than strictly necessary.

"Only me, darling," Alichia said and opened the door fully. She had a steaming mug in one hand. "I didn't want to wake you, if you were asleep."

"I wasn't."

"No, so I can see. Thunder and lightning can be daunting to even the bravest. But I was wondering if maybe a cup of hot chocolate might cheer you up?"

She said it as if it was going to be our little secret.

It was very nice of her, of course, but the soup and the tea were already sloshing around my tummy, and I didn't fancy anything else. I just couldn't think of a polite way to say no.

"Er, thanks..." I said. Mostly so as not to hurt her feelings.

She came right inside, put the mug on the bedside table and sat down on the edge of my bed.

"How was your Tridecimal, darling?" she asked and patted my hand. "Was it exciting?"

The question made me feel guilty. All those animals, all those eyes... I'd promised to help, but I was no closer to finding out how, despite everything that had happened.

"It was... fine," I said. I sipped my cocoa like a good girl, but was really wishing she would leave. Not because she wasn't being nice, because she was – awfully nice, in fact – but I thought that business with the leeches was gross, and it was hard not to think that the hand now patting me also liked stroking leeches. It was like the few times I'd met someone who wanted to be my friend more than I wanted to be theirs – it made me feel sort of embarrassed and guilty even while I was wishing they would just go away.

Alichia was in no hurry to leave – she seemed to have all the time in the world.

"What animal did you meet?"

"There were... several."

"Really? Well, that happens sometimes. Were you frightened?"

"Not really."

She sighed.

"Well, I think we are making our wildwitch children grow up much too soon." Suddenly she looked so sad that I felt even more guilty about wanting her to leave. Perhaps she was lonely. I mean, there must be a limit to how many thrilling conversations you can have with a leech.

"Do you have children?" I asked.

"One. That's to say... I had... I had a daughter. She was your age when she... disappeared."

"I'm sorry to hear that."

I remembered the picture in the house on stilts. A girl with blonde hair like Alichia's and eyes almost the same shade of raisin-brown. That must be her – the missing daughter.

And then something clicked into place. Tridecimal Night. Fair hair and brown eyes. Mum's voice:

"Her name was Lia. Her mother was also a wildwitch, but Lia wasn't sure if she wanted to be one herself. She... she was a gentle girl, a little insecure at times, but brave in her own way. We always stuck together and so no one ever really teased us. She had brown eyes like you, but very fair hair."

Was that her? If so, she hadn't just disappeared. She'd been killed. Eaten alive. Eaten by the animal she'd tried to help.

Did I remind her of Lia? Was that why she was sitting here, stroking my hand, being nice? I didn't like to ask. But I drank a little more of my cocoa, and smiled cautiously.

"Thank you," I said. "Now I don't feel scared any more."

"I'm glad," she said, patting my hand again. "Sleep tight, darling."

I didn't think I'd be able to fall asleep as long as there was thunder and lightning across Westmark. But my eyelids grew heavy, in fact my whole body grew heavier and heavier until at last I was asleep.

When I woke up, I couldn't remember where I was.

I wasn't properly awake, and my body felt as if I had gained about twenty-five kilos in my sleep. The duvet covering me was like a damp sack of cement pushing me down into the mattress, and it wasn't until I heard the distant rumble of thunder that I remembered the storm, Westmark, Alichia and the leeches.

I fumbled for the light switch, and I found it, but nothing happened when I pressed it. The ancient wiring in the house seemed to have given up the unequal fight against the storm.

I knew there were candles, candlesticks and matches on the chest of drawers next to my bed, but when I reached out my hand, I almost knocked over the cocoa mug.

Finally I found the matches and managed to light a candle. And that was when I spotted it. Or rather, spotted them.

Up my arm in an almost straight line, there were five round marks. And inside each of them, I could clearly see the little "Y"-shaped bite marks left behind by a leech.

CHAPTER FOURTEEN

The Bloodling Awakens

Yuuuuck. I rubbed my arm as if I could erase the bites. Yuck, yuck, yuck. How did I get those?

It must be Alichia. It had to be. Unless I'd been walking in my sleep and ended up in some swamp, which was highly unlikely, so it must be her doing. And I'd felt sorry for her and drunk her cocoa and let her pat my hand... *Yuck.*

Perhaps that explained why everything felt so leaden? The duvet, my arms, my legs?

And if she had done it, then why? I wasn't ill. I didn't need to be treated with leeches.

I struggled out of bed. I had to find Aunt Isa this instant. But where was her room?

I cursed Westmark for being old and big enough to offer guest rooms to a whole army. And I cursed Alichia, who'd insisted it was no trouble at all to make up beds in separate rooms. Had she done it on purpose? So that I'd been alone, and she could put her disgusting leeches on me?

I staggered across the floor to the door. I was perfectly capable of walking, I told myself. My legs might weigh more than usual, but I could do it! When I realized how dark the passage was, I decided to go back to fetch the candlestick and luckily my legs seemed to get a little more mobile with every step I took.

"Aunt Isa?" It was difficult to whisper and shout at the same time, but I didn't want to raise my voice too much in case Alichia heard me. I didn't fancy bumping into her right now. "Aunt Isa!"

There was no reply, neither from my aunt – nor Alichia, luckily. I tiptoed along the passage on bare feet until I reached the next room and listened by the door. I recognized the loud snoring straight away – Oscar.

I ran into his room and over to his bed. He lay flat on his back with his mouth open, sleeping just as soundly as he always did.

"Oscar!" I shook him.

"Shaummmreubjsf," he said, or something to that effect. Whatever it was, it didn't make any sense.

There was a mug of cocoa on his bedside table too. Unlike me, he'd drunk all of his. Now it was true that Oscar always slept as if drugged, but I was starting to get a really bad feeling about this. I grabbed his right arm and held the candle to it in order to study it more closely. No round "Y" marks. Well, that was a good start, although Oscar would probably just have thought it was "super-cool" and complain that he hadn't been awake while it happened.

I shook him again, and he seemed to wake up a little.

"Whaawhaaassupp?" he said, which I was pretty sure meant: what's up?

"Look," I said, stretching out my arm. "I've been bitten!"

He blinked. His eyes were narrow slits, but he was awake now.

"Coooool," he mumbled and closed his eyes again. "Good for you..."

"No. No, it really isn't. I didn't do it on purpose. It was Alichia. It must've been. She made them bite me!"

"Why-would-she-do-that?" He still sounded rather drowsy, but his eyes opened a tiny crack again.

"How would I know? She's gross. Perhaps she just likes watching them bite people? Or maybe..." I remembered her sad look and her hand patting mine. "... Maybe she has some freaky plan to kidnap me..."

In my mind's eye I saw a horror movie where Alichia dressed me in her dead daughter's clothes and pretended that I was Lia. She'd called me "darling" the whole time.

"Why?" Oscar said again, more clearly this time. "I mean, why would she do that?"

"The woman's mad. She doesn't need a reason. And *I* don't want to be here a minute longer. We need to find Aunt Isa and get out of here."

"What about Shanaia?"

He had a point. If Alichia really was crazy, she could have done anything to Shanaia.

"OK," I said. "Let's start with Shanaia. At least we know where her room is."

I thought Oscar took forever putting on his jumper and his shoes. I looked down at my own bare feet, and wondered if I should nip back and get my boots, but my body felt itchy and impatient with worry. We had to get going. Onwards – not back.

W hen I opened the door to Shanaia's bedroom, we were met by an icy blast of wind that blew out my candle. The big window overlooking the sea was wide open, and rain splashed onto the floor with every new gust of wind. Shanaia was lying on her side in the old four-poster bed, and most of her bed linen had slipped down onto the wet floor.

I couldn't relight the candle because I hadn't been smart enough to bring the matches. But the clouds no longer covered the moon completely and the blue glow that fell through the open window was bright enough for us to see at least some of the room.

"Close the window," I said to Oscar.

On the mantelpiece there was a lighter, one of those gas ones with an on-off button and a long tip, so you don't burn your fingers when you try to light a fire. I used it to relight my candle.

"Shanaia," I called out, not really thinking that she would reply. I was expecting her to be at least as hard to rouse as Oscar.

"Aunt Abbie?" she mumbled in a very frail, almost childish voice.

"It's Clara and Oscar," I said. Shanaia's Aunt Abigael had been dead for years. She'd looked after Shanaia when she lost her parents, and it seemed ominous that Shanaia was calling for her aunt as if she were still alive. But then she half sat up in bed and looked at us with eyes even blacker and darker than usual.

"Clara," she said. "Sorry. I was in the middle of a dream. It felt so real..." She sounded sad, as if waking up distressed her. "What are you doing here? I'm sorry I didn't come to your Tridecimal, but I..." Suddenly she shook her head. "Something's wrong with me. I feel really weird. I sleep the whole time and..."

"If you insist on sleeping with the window wide open in the middle of the storm, no wonder you get ill," Oscar said.

"I had to open it so Kitti could get in and out. But... Kitti. Where is she? Is she outside?"

All three of us looked at the stand next to the fireplace. There was no kestrel on the perch, but there was a small, feathery body on the floor.

"*Noooo!*" Shanaia screamed at the top of her voice, and I knew why. My heart, too, almost stopped; it was only a few months since Shanaia had lost her old wild-friend, the ferret Elfrida, which Chimera had killed.

Shanaia jumped out of bed, wobbled and fell onto one knee, got up again, and threw herself on the floor next to the body of the kestrel. She scooped it up and held it close to her chest.

"Is she...?" I could hear that Oscar was afraid to ask the question.

But Shanaia shook her head.

"No. She's alive. She's asleep... but... why doesn't she wake up? And why...?" She nodded towards the floor where Kitti had been lying.

It takes a lot for a sleeping kestrel to fall off its perch. No wonder Shanaia had thought that Kitti was dead.

Then I remembered the bowl of bloody meat scraps which Alichia had been kind enough to prepare for the kestrel. I was pretty sure kestrels didn't drink hot chocolate.

"It's Alichia," I said, totally convinced now that I was right. "I think she's drugged everyone in the house."

"Alichia?" Shanaia was baffled. "Why on earth would she do that? She's only come here to help..."

"That's what you think. When did you send for her?"

"I don't think I did. But so many animals here were bitten by leeches and it made them unwell, so I sent Kitti with a message for the Raven Mothers. Soon afterwards I was bitten myself, but fortunately Alichia turned up and was ever so helpful. She said that the Raven Mothers had sent her."

"Thuja never said anything about that." And she surely wouldn't have told us that Alichia was at home if she'd known that she was with Shanaia. Thuja could have saved us the walk across the wetlands and sent us straight to Westmark instead!

Shanaia shook her head in disbelief.

"Clara, you must be mistaken. She's been looking after me while I've been ill; she's taken care of everything..."

"Yes, I'm sure she has," I said. "She has taken care of everything so she could get everything the way *she* wanted."

"But what are you accusing her of, Clara? And why?"

I couldn't explain it so I held up my arm and showed her my bites.

"Look," I said. "I got those while I was asleep. And I don't suppose that leeches wander around the house on their own? As far as I know they're better at swimming than walking."

Shanaia studied the bites.

"OK, now that *is* weird," she conceded.

"Where were you bitten?"

"On my leg." She pulled up her pyjama bottoms and showed me her marks. "Five times, just like you."

I stared at Shanaia's calf. Not so much at the marks, which were dark against her pale skin, but more because...

"Shanaia. Are you getting *spots*?" Faint, green blotches had started to spread up and down her legs, and they reminded me of something.

"Alichia said that leech fever could result in changes to skin pigmentation..." Shanaia said.

"That's more than changes to skin pigmentation," I said. "And if you're not careful, you'll end up like Fredric!"

"Fredric?" Shanaia was struggling to catch up.

"He looks like a frog," Oscar said. "He lives with Alichia, and he looks like a frog. Or perhaps... more like a leech..."

And to think that I'd felt sorry for Alichia for having to put up with miserable, old Fredric... no wonder he was in such a bad mood, what with his landlady turning him into a leech and all.

"But if she is to blame for the leech bites," Oscar said, "what about Kahla and your dad? That couldn't have been Alichia."

I mulled it over.

"Why not?" I then said. "Just because we didn't see her, doesn't mean she wasn't there."

"Not if she was here..."

"Was she?" I asked Shanaia. "Was she with you all day yesterday and the day before?"

"I don't know," she said. "I've been asleep pretty much the whole time..."

"So she could have done it," I insisted. "She could have used the wildways. She could have crept up on Kahla, either at home or on her way to Aunt Isa. You can't see a thing in the wildways fog. And you don't feel leech bites until later."

"But what about your dad?" Oscar objected. "Surely he would have seen her? She's not exactly someone you'd miss in those clothes, and there was no wildways fog for her to hide in when he was bitten."

Colours, my dad had said when I found him. *Colours everywhere. Why is everything turning red?*

"Maybe he did see her," I said. "Maybe that explains why he was muttering about colours – he caught a glimpse of her before she... did whatever she did." A wildwitch could do all kinds of things to an unsuspecting ordinary person like my dad. Perhaps she'd twisted his life cord. That could easily knock you unconscious; I'd seen Chimera do it once to Bumble. "Where else could those leeches have come from? Do we know anybody who farms them except her?"

"No," Oscar conceded. "Only I still can't see why she'd want to do it."

"We can worry about that later," I said. "Shanaia, can you walk? More than a few steps, I mean?"

"I guess so," she said, although we could see she still wasn't feeling very well. "Why?"

"Because we need to find Aunt Isa, and then we need to get out of here before this leech plague finishes us off."

"I think you're being overdramatic now," Shanaia said.

"Why? You should have seen Fredric. He can't walk any more. His skin is leech-coloured practically all over. She was supposed to help him get better, he paid her lots of money to do it, but he's been getting steadily worse. Because *good old* Alichia has been ever so helpful."

Shanaia looked at Kitti, still lying limp and drugged in her hands.

"Perhaps you're right," she said.

A violent gust of wind made the ceiling beams creak and groan and then we heard another bang somewhere below us. But this time it wasn't a clap of thunder.

"That was the front door slamming," Shanaia said. "Did no one shut it properly against the storm?"

She went over to the window and looked outside. I followed her.

A windswept figure, with petticoats, shawl and the ends of her headscarf flapping like wings in the wind, was walking along the path that led to the beach. A torch beam flitted across the trees, the path and the rocks. There was no doubt it was Alichia – but where was she going?

"She's heading for the cave," Aunt Isa said, without a trace of doubt in her voice.

She was already awake when we rushed in with our bites and leech stories. Her cocoa sat completely untouched on the bedside table, and she didn't seem nearly as surprised as we'd expected.

"I had a feeling that something was wrong here," she said. "Only I didn't know what."

Outside in the rain Hoot-Hoot was flying silently above Alichia's head, and she never noticed him. But his presence explained why Aunt Isa was so sure that she knew where the leech witch was going.

"Why would she go there?" Shanaia wondered. "I don't think there are any leeches there..."

An icy sensation started somewhere at the back of my neck and spread down my spine, and from there to my whole body.

"No," I said. "There are no leeches. But there's something else."

Solid rock boiled and turned molten once more; it burst and exploded; red-hot drops of melted glass sprayed the walls of the cave in hissing cascades.

Bravita escaping from her prison.

My dream, my nightmare had returned to me in vivid detail. Every single drop of melted glass, every hiss, and in particular, the captive's boundless, incandescent, indomitable rage. It flushed through me like a fever, and I didn't know if what I'd seen was the past, the present or the future, I only knew that it was real. There was no way this was just a dream.

"Bravita..." I whispered. "The Bloodling, she's waking up..."

"What are you saying?" Aunt Isa whispered, and froze.

"She's been trapped down there," I said in a voice that didn't sound like mine. "For four hundred years. Under the floor of the cave, trapped in the solidified stone. Ever since she and Viridian fought, and they both lost. It's her..." I had to pause for breath, but I was sure that I was right. "*She*'s the revenant. *She* wants to live again. And five drops of the right blood can open her prison."

I looked down at my arm. At the five circular marks. Surely each leech could hold much more than just a single drop.

"Yours?" Aunt Isa said. "Your blood?"

I gulped, and then I nodded.

"Mine. Or rather, Viridian's..." Somehow I must be related to Viridian, be "of her blood", as she would probably have put it. "Why it's mine, rather than Mum's or yours, I don't know. But ever since Chimera first tried getting her talons into me, this is what it's all been about – opening Bravita Bloodling's prison."

CHAPTER FIFTEEN

Heart Blood

"We won't make it," Shanaia panted. "I'm too slow!"

Shanaia was wheezing badly, and it was obvious that she couldn't move faster than she already was. The wind lashed the rain into our faces, and all four of us were soaked to the skin in a matter of minutes.

"Even if we left you behind, we still wouldn't make it," Aunt Isa said. She had to shout to make herself heard over the storm that was shaking the trees and making them creak. "Not like this. She's too far ahead of us. We'll have to cheat. So – take each other's hands and hold on tight."

I grabbed Oscar's hand and he took Shanaia's.

"The wildways?" he shouted to me.

I nodded. There was no gradual transition, no gentle wildsong or humming. Aunt Isa expelled an operatic scream, so piercing, violent and powerful it hurt my eardrums and my wildsense. With a sudden jolt we found ourselves in the middle of the wildways fog.

With another jolt just as sudden, the others disappeared from me.

A violent pain shot up my right arm as if the five leech bites were five, red-hot demon fingers. Oscar's hand was torn from my grasp, I couldn't hold on.

The noise of the storm faded away. It was silent here. It was grey, foggy and desolate. And I was alone.

I felt a panicky pounding in my chest. Possibly my heart.

Alone on the wildways. That could kill you. Especially when you were a thirteen-year-old, almost untrained wildwitch who still couldn't find her own way around. Even Kahla had her dad to take her to and from Aunt Isa's house every day for her lessons.

I'd been here once before. And if Cat hadn't found me, it would probably have cost me my life.

Cat. *I'll see you again. But not until you really need me.*

Surely that time was now?

"Cat!"

The fog simply swallowed my voice. There was no echo, and I had a feeling that the sound travelled only a short distance.

"Cat..." I called out again. "I really, really need you..."

Nothing happened. There was no reply; I didn't have the faintest sensation that he was out there somewhere or that he'd heard me and was on his way.

He'd promised. He'd promised to come back. I didn't know whether to get angrier or even more scared. *I have to go now*, he'd said, as if deep down he didn't want to, but he had no choice.

I couldn't even begin to imagine that someone or something could force Cat to do anything he didn't want to, but what if... what if something was controlling Cat? What if he actually wanted to help me – but couldn't?

The damp grey cold crept slowly into my body. It filled my nose and my mouth, and it reached my bones so my skeleton felt icy under my flesh and muscles.

Then something tugged at me.

I spun around, looking about me wildly, but I was still alone. Although the touch had been noticeable and real, it hadn't been a physical tug.

Was that Aunt Isa trying to reach me?

I closed my eyes in order to sense better. I could see my own eyelids, the fine web of veins under the skin like a red light, warmer and stronger than the desolate world of the wildways. There *was* something, something that could reach me, something that could show me the way. A thin, red thread through the labyrinthine fog.

I followed the thread. With my eyes still closed, I walked through the fog, and the red light grew stronger. I heard a voice, warm and loving it seemed to me, a voice that was humming and singing.

"Blood from the north, ancestral blood, those who don't remember, yet who are..."

A drop of blood fell, dark red and viscous at the start of its fall, then thinner and brighter as gravity dragged it down.

"Blood from the south, enemy blood, she who feigns friendship, but is no one's friend..."

Another red drop trailed through the air, and this time I thought I could almost see where it fell. It hit a rock and some damp sand at the edge of a pattern I knew well.

"Blood from the east, foreigner's blood, he who plays the wise man, but knows little..."

Now why was I suddenly reminded of Fredric? He had nothing to do with any of this; all he did was sit in his wheelchair, hating the world. And yet the image of his surly face refused to go away.

"Blood from the west, homestead blood, she who guards here, yet is weak..."

Who guards here?

I felt something under my feet, which wasn't fog or the wildways. Rocky ground. The cave. Westmark. I opened my eyes.

The thunder sounded muffled and remote, but the sharp white flash of lightning seared through the cracks and openings and showed me Alichia's ample figure in the middle of the grotto, at the centre of the wheel pattern in the floor. She'd pulled up her petticoats and bunched them around her hips, and it looked as if she was wearing a pair of bloomers made from a thick, dark and strangely fraying fabric. I didn't realize until the next flash of lightning that the fabric was alive. From ankles to groin, her legs were totally covered in leeches. Fat leeches, thin leeches, black leeches, brown leeches, striped and shiny, dark and matte, they clustered so densely I couldn't catch a single glimpse of white-skinned flesh.

She bent down with great tenderness and picked one up.

"Come on, darling," she whispered. "It's your turn now."

It released its hold obediently. Alichia hummed to it, and gently stroked the swollen rings that made up its body.

"Heart blood," she whispered. "At the centre of the world, at the centre of the wheel, she who bound the others and was in turn bound herself. Viridian's blood shall open that which Viridian herself once locked. Bloodling, do you hear me? It is Alichia calling you! Give me your power and grant me my revenge!"

Somewhere behind my forehead there was a red roar. My arm, the arm with the leech bites, was stinging so badly and felt so hot that I half expected to see flames. Alichia carried on, stroking the leech, and blood started dripping from its mouth...

One drop fell. And then another. And then a third and a fourth.

"Stop!" I called out, taking a few wobbly steps towards her. "Alichia, what are you doing?"

She made a half turn towards me, and she didn't look surprised. It was as if she'd been expecting me.

"Turn and turn about," she said with a perfectly straight face. "Your mum will feel it now. Now *she* too will know what it's like to lose a daughter."

And the fifth drop fell.

I could almost see it hover in the air. As if it fought gravity, refusing to fall. But it did fall. And it carried on falling. And it hit the stone floor, right in the hub of the wheel.

YEEEEeeeeeeeeeeeeeeeeeeeeessssssssssssssssssss.......

I heard the scream even though it was silent – and I knew who'd made it. I knew that Bravita Bloodling was suspended under my feet, frozen and trapped like an insect in a piece of amber. I also knew what would happen next, it was just like my dream.

The congealed mass of rock beneath my feet split. Cracks appeared and spread across its surface. In a roar of wildpower the trapped revenant straightened her body, hunched and bowed for four hundred years, and shattered her prison into smithereens. Solid rock boiled and turned molten once more; it burst and exploded; red-hot drops of melted glass sprayed the walls of the cave in hissing cascades.

A drop hit my shoulder and burned straight through my jumper and T-shirt. My skin burned. I could smell it. I could smell my own scorched flesh.

Something burst up through the floor. It couldn't be a human body because its flesh and blood would have burned up exactly like my shoulder was burning now. It couldn't be a human body, but it looked like one. She glowed red in the darkness – then white and black when a flash of lightning struck – then red again. The heat rolled towards me as if someone had opened the doors to a hundred ovens at once. At first her eyes were black, then red, then black again. Her hair wasn't hair, but flames that flared up only to disappear and leave behind a naked scalp. She didn't even notice that the heat made Alichia's petticoats catch fire, she didn't hear Alichia scream. She saw only me.

"Viridian..." she hissed between lips that couldn't be flesh and blood, and yet looked it. "I'm taking your blood. I'm taking it now."

I wanted to protest. I wanted to tell her that I wasn't Viridian, that I was a thirteen-year-old girl who happened to have a few drops of Viridian's blood inside her. But I knew she wouldn't care. And I knew that unless I did something very soon, I would die here in the flames, and my blood would give the Bloodling the life she yearned for.

Once before I'd stood inside heartfire without burning up. Once before I'd survived trial by wildfire. My swollen eyelids couldn't close, and perhaps it was better that I carried on seeing. But I was looking more inwards than outwards and I retrieved my memory of the firebird's laughter from my wildwitch mind.

"Help me," I whispered, still more inwards than outwards. "I'm Clara, and I'm calling you."

A playful heat enveloped me and briefly pushed back the destructive, all-consuming flames. Even my shoulder stopped hurting.

Who are you? This new fire asked, but in a friendly tone of voice.

"I'm Clara. I'm a wildwitch. I speak the truth or keep silent. And I never take without giving."

The firebird laughed. Its laughter was like a whirl-wind of tiny flame feathers that spread through the cave, and where they landed, the hungry fire died down. The boiling masses of stone began to cool. The floor started to solidify.

Bravita froze too, but only for a second or so. Her gaze released mine and shifted instead to the firebird flying through the cave in a vortex of flame feathers and laughter. I couldn't take my eyes off it. It was so gentle and so strong at the same time, wild but friendly, real but magical, an animal, a bird, yes, but so much more than that.

I was so busy watching its flight that I didn't see what happened. All I saw was something dark and heavy hurtle through the air; striking the bird's body, crushing its delicate ribs with a sudden, crisp little snap.

The firebird's light flickered. It plunged to the ground. I reached out my hands to catch it, but the thing that landed light and warm in my palms was already dead. The flame feathers around us went out one by one like dying embers. And Bravita grew in size and wrenched first one foot, then the other free from the congealing rock.

She had thrown a stone at it. Not a curse or something violent and magical. A simple stone had killed my firebird, and all its gentle wildness had been snuffed out like a candle.

I struggled to understand it.

Struggled to understand how it could die so easily, but I found it even harder to understand why someone would want to kill it. Why someone would throw a rock at something so beautiful, and throw it hard, accurately and without mercy.

Bravita took a step towards me, and I knew what she wanted. She was the hungry one. She was the revenant. She needed life in order to live. She'd taken the life of the firebird, and now she was going to take mine – *the confused life of a foolish thirteen-year-old girl.*

And I didn't see that there was any way I could stop her.

CHAPTER SIXTEEN

Adiuvate!

"**S**top, Bloodling..."

The words weren't mine. Nor did they come from Alichia, who was kneeling on the floor some distance from me, wailing as she tried to cool her burns with water from the stream that ran through the cave. So who could it be?

Bravita stopped as if she were a horse that had been reined in. She turned towards the sound and saw what I saw:

A giant black cat with very yellow eyes.

"Nightclaw..." she snarled.

Cat hadn't spoken either. His voice was silent and could be heard only in my mind. But there was someone by his side... I thought I could almost see... she was transparent, not clearly visible, and yet... a woman was there, and yet at the same time she wasn't. And she was the one Bravita was looking at.

"Viridian..." she said, and the woman's figure seemed to become more visible. "Where have you been hiding these last four hundred years?"

"Bloodling. Stop. You and I don't belong here. Don't you understand? The world has moved on without us. When something is dead, it ought to stay dead."

It was as if Bravita hadn't heard her.

"It's the cat, isn't it?" she said. "He's carried you. You've lived inside him like a ghost. You're his tenth life. No wonder he had to keep growing."

Cat sat down languidly and started licking a front paw. He didn't say anything, didn't do anything that wasn't feline. Nightclaw. That had been the name of Viridian's wildfriend, I remembered. Did that really explain Cat? Why he was the way he was, and why he could do the things he could? Was he Nightclaw?

"It's time to let go," Viridian said. "For both of us. I'll go to the grave with you, if that's any consolation."

"I've no intention of going to any grave," Bravita said, and her black eyes smouldered. She was naked and completely smooth, as if her body consisted of solidified rock, and perhaps it did. Surely nothing else could have survived that heat. "But I'll certainly help *you* get there."

Something whispered to me deep inside, where Bravita wouldn't be able to hear it. I wasn't sure if it was Viridian's voice or Cat's. Perhaps it was both of them.

Remember the sword? Remember the sword with which you severed Chimera's wings?

I don't think I'd ever be able to forget that. Only there hadn't been a sword, at least not a visible one. Only something incredibly sharp and cold and painful, which cut its way out of me and into Chimera. But Chimera's wings had fallen, first one, then the other, and the stolen bird-lives used to create them had been set free.

That sword is you, Clara.

No. I almost shook my head, but stopped myself just in time. Right now Bravita's attention was on Cat and Viridian's semi-transparent figure, and not me. And I would very much like for that to continue.

I know you don't believe me, but it's the truth. I gave you knowledge, but I can't give you power. Power requires life, and I have no more lives left. Find the sword. Find it inside yourself. And use it. Or the Bloodling will go out into the world and take whatever she wants.

The floor in the cave had taken on a red glow again, and if I narrowed my sore eyelids, I could see the lines of the wheel drawn in thin, red threads, threads of blood. North, south, east, west. Ancestral blood, enemy blood, foreigner's blood and homestead blood. I was standing in a web of blood magic and, though I didn't want it to be this way, it might be what I was best at, what I understood the best because it was in my blood. Cat got up and started walking towards Bravita. Viridian followed like a luminous shadow by his side.

Bravita hesitated as if she didn't know what to do with the dead woman and the cat.

Then Cat took off in a mighty leap. He grew in the air, getting bigger and bigger, the size of a panther, a lion, bigger still. Bravita raised her hands the second before he reached her stony throat, and the next second all of her being was focused on him.

Now... the voice in my mind whispered. *Take her now!*

If only I could get that moment back.

If only I could have a second try.

Why can't life be like that? Why does it just carry on without us being able to fix anything? Without us being able to make amends, without us being able to right what we did wrong?

I should have done to her what I did to Chimera – lunged at her with that inner sword, that sharp, cold power I had inside me. I should have done it at that moment.

I hesitated too long.

I didn't believe in it.

It wasn't until Cat screamed his cat cry and blazed up in a scarlet explosion of fire, blood and bones; it wasn't until then that I charged. It wasn't until then that I struck.

"Let go of what doesn't belong to you!"

I think I was screaming it out loud; I certainly thought I did. I struck at Bravita's rock-hard chest, once, twice... and the third time my hands went straight through her as if I really were holding a sword, a sword strong enough to cut through solid rock.

"Let go!" I screamed. "Let go, let go, let go!"

I wanted her to let go of Cat. I wanted her to let go of life.

She was no longer there.

Her body, which could never have been flesh and blood, though it had appeared it was... shattered into a thousand pieces as though it had been made not of rock, but of glass. Bloodling shards flew everywhere, shattering against the walls of the cave and falling to the floor with a dull clatter... Her hungry soul reached out for me, trying to get inside me. It felt as if something was slamming into me, howling, trying to gain access, scratching, rending, tearing at me, trying to force its way into my body, my head and my heart.

"Clara!"

It was Aunt Isa's voice. I heard it. And yet at the same time I didn't. I fought back as hard as I could. I tried desperately to make Bravita release me, yet I could feel how she was starting to penetrate deeper and deeper, seeping into every cut and scratch, entering in wherever she found weakness and doubt. I couldn't let her win. She mustn't be allowed to return to life through me. I pressed my hands against my chest as if trying to rip her out of me with my bare hands, although I knew it was impossible.

Instead I felt something else. Something round, smooth and as warm as my body – Mr Malkin's gift to me, the pretty little witchwheel.

Even grown-up wildwitches sometimes need help. And this wasn't something I could handle on my own. The word appeared in my mouth as if it had been waiting for me to utter it: "**Adiuvate!**"

Come to my rescue.

Help me, before she takes something bigger and more important than my life.

I started to black out. Breathing became more and more difficult. I think I fell, but I didn't feel myself hitting the ground. I'd called for help, but I didn't know if anyone had heard me.

CHAPTER SEVENTEEN

Zombie

"Clara, Clara, please wake up."

I was back home in my own bed. Mum was trying to wake me up. I guess I was going to school, but... I felt strangely ill.

"Clara!!"

No, hang on. It wasn't Mum. It was Oscar. And I wasn't back in my bed.

My eyelids felt thick and heavy, and I knew without checking that my eyelashes were gone. They'd been burned off, along with most of my eyebrows. I ached everywhere both inside and out, so much that I almost couldn't bear being alive. I had a headache and I felt sick. But I wasn't hungry.

I wasn't hungry.

It was absolutely incredible how much better I felt, despite the pain. Because if Bravita had won, then surely I would now be feeling so hungry that I'd have eaten anything living that came near me.

Wherever she was now, she wasn't inside me.

I forced my eyes open.

Oscar was kneeling beside me. His face was deathly pale under the freckles and, for once, he didn't look as if he thought everything was super-cool.

"You're not dead, are you?" he asked. "Please tell me you're not a zombie?"

"No," I croaked. "I think I'm still me. I don't fancy eating your brain – or anything else, in case you were wondering."

"Phew," he said. "In that case, please would you sit up and try looking a bit more alive?"

I sat up.

We were still in the cave. It was quiet apart from the soft whisper of the stream, and the light spilling through the cracks in the roof of the cave was no longer lightning but daylight.

Five figures were lying around me in a loose sort of circle. Aunt Isa, Mr Malkin, Mrs Pommerans, Master Millaconda and Shanaia. None of them said anything. None of them was moving.

"Aunt Isa?"

She didn't react. Oscar sniffed.

"They don't move," he said. "I can't even see them breathe. But their eyes are open. It's super-spooky..."

I struggled to get up on my feet. He was right. They were lying very still, staring into the air as if...

As if bewitched.

Aunt Isa's face was frozen in a fierce, determined grimace, Shanaia's eyes were huge and anxious, Master Millaconda's dark eyebrows were frowning so much they almost met. From Mr Malkin's waistcoat pocket a nervous little squeak could be heard, and a nose and a pair of long whiskers quivered faintly along the edge of the pocket before disappearing back into the hiding place. Mrs Pommerans looked neither gentle nor kind right now, but decidedly angry. And not one of them moved a muscle.

I tentatively touched Aunt Isa's shoulder. It felt like the shoulder of a doll, hard and stiff. I shook her harder.

"Aunt Isa!"

"It's no use," Oscar said glumly. "I've tried. I shouted and I've shaken them. They won't wake up. Or at least I can't wake them."

"What happened?" I could barely get the words out.

Oscar rubbed his nose and sniffed again. He wasn't crying any more, but I think he had been. His eyes were a little red.

"I... I really did try to hold onto you," he said. "On the wildways..."

"I know. It wasn't you. It was me that couldn't hold on."

"I wanted us to look for you, but Isa said stopping Alichia was more important. That we would have to look for you afterwards."

I nodded. "And she was right," I said. I stared down at poor Aunt Isa, still lying immobile and staring. Could she hear us? I had no idea. What if she was aware of everything that was going on, but unable to move?

"We followed Alichia through the entrance to the cave as quickly as we could. But then we heard loud crashes and a lot of... crackling, as if something was burning, and it got so hot that we couldn't move forward without... without us catching fire. And when the fire – or whatever it was – went out, all we could see was you and Alichia, and Alichia was kneeling in the brook, wailing and howling because she'd been burned. And you were standing... you were standing up, looking completely out of it. You were flailing your arms and twisting and... it was really creepy. As if you were possessed or something."

"I very nearly was," I said. "Bravita tried to... move into me."

"And you were screaming some weird word..."

"Adiuvate..." I whispered.

"And suddenly... suddenly they were all here. I mean, Isa and Shanaia were already here, but the other three came crashing out of nowhere, and your aunt grabbed hold of me and practically threw me on the ground next to you, and hissed: 'Stay there!' in that voice... you know the one where you think she'll turn you into something nasty if you don't do as you're told... and then they formed a circle" – he pointed to the prostrate figures – "and started singing at the top of their voices."

"What were they singing? Could you make out any words?"

"No. I mean, it was obviously some kind of wild-song, wasn't it? And then you let out a scream... or rather, it was coming from you, but it didn't *sound* like you. And then you collapsed in a heap and you didn't get up. And the next moment... or no. They keeled over. At exactly the same time, as if they were somehow connected... I... I didn't know what to do."

I stepped into the centre of the circle. Then I put my hand on the small wheel ornament around my neck and said tentatively: "You can stop now. I... I'm me again. She's gone."

Nothing happened. They didn't stir, they didn't reply, they didn't breathe, at least not so that we could see it. I squatted down on my haunches next to Aunt Isa and touched her shoulder again. I wondered if I should try a bit of wildsinging?

"Aunt Isa... please... please come back?"

"I've tried everything," Oscar said. "I even slapped Shanaia across the face. You know, like they do in the movies when people faint or get hysterical. She didn't move and I just ended up with sore fingers."

"What about Cat? Have you seen him?"

Oscar shook his head. "No."

"Or... a kind of ghost? A woman?"

Oscar's eyes widened.

"No," he said. "Is this place haunted?"

"I don't know," I said. "Perhaps it was... but it isn't now. What happened to Alichia?" Because I could see she was no longer in the grotto.

"She crawled out. Or rather – she tried. There was a rockfall. I think she was buried under it."

"Where?"

"In the passage along the brook."

For the first time I realized that the floor in the grotto was much wetter than usual. And that the water level was rising.

I took a few unsteady steps in the direction of the exit. When Oscar said there'd been a rockfall, he wasn't kidding. It looked as if most of the roof had collapsed, and the reason the water was rising was because the brook could no longer follow its normal course through the grotto and out into the sea.

If even the water couldn't get out... then what about us?

"Oscar," I said. "Does that mean... that we're trapped here?"

"I'm afraid we are," he said. "Unless you know another way out of here?"

CHAPTER EIGHTEEN

Daylight

"Can't we just travel by those wildways thingies?" Oscar asked. "I was kind of hoping you could sort that out when you woke up."

I shook my head.

"I'm sorry, but... I'm just not skilled enough. I don't know how it's done."

"But you always..."

"No," I said rather brusquely. "Not without help." Cat... Nightclaw. Why did I feel utterly hopeless whenever I thought about him? It was as if I were sure that I'd never see him again.

I had made several feeble attempts to rouse Aunt Isa and the others with wildsong but it hadn't had the slightest effect. Perhaps I just wasn't good enough. Or perhaps not even the wildest wildwitch would have been able to wake them. What was it Aunt Isa had said about zombies? *Poor, confused souls so affected by poison and witchcraft that they no longer know if they're dead or alive.* I didn't think that Aunt Isa and the others had been poisoned, but they were trapped by some kind of witchcraft, and it was difficult to tell if they were dead or alive, and although I'd sung my heart out, they were no more alive than they were before.

"I'm hungry," Oscar said. "And it's a horrible feeling. I think starving to death must be a terrible..."

"Stop it. We're not going to starve to death."

"We are if we don't get out of here..."

For a while we sat next to each other, equally despondent.

Then suddenly Oscar slapped his hand against his forehead.

"Doh..." he said. "Now I know why you don't fancy eating my brain."

"What? What are you on about?"

"Then again... who says smart brains taste better than stupid ones..."

"Oscar, get a grip!"

He grinned from ear to ear.

"Daylight," he said. "There's a gap up there, and a very nice big one at that, or there wouldn't be this much light down here."

I looked up. The cave ceiling wasn't like the ceiling in a house. What I could see was spiky and rugged, and stalactites hung like icicles in large, grey clusters. It was true that there was light from above, but you couldn't see the hole it was coming from. And the tips of the nearest stalactites were many metres above us.

"Yes, OK, there's a hole," I conceded. "But I don't see how we're going to get up there."

"Hello," he said. "Have you forgotten that I'm the school wall-climbing champion?"

He fell twice. The first time wasn't too bad, he was only about two metres up, and he pretty much landed on his feet. But the second time...

"Oscar..."

He lay completely still on his back with his mouth open and his arm flailing helplessly.

"... I... can't..." he groaned.

He couldn't breathe. I sat down beside him and raised his shoulders and head a little. I took a deep breath and did my best to sing something that sounded like wildsong. Although it hadn't worked on Aunt Isa and Shanaia and the others, perhaps it would work better on a living boy. Or rather... a boy who didn't look like a zombie. And Aunt Isa always said that the melody wasn't important, it was just a way of harnessing your power, the way a magnifying glass gathers light. I hummed some rather false and disjointed notes, and *wished* with all my heart that Oscar would get better.

I'm not sure if it worked, but he suddenly took a deep, gasping breath and started to cough, splutter and hawk.

"I was... winded..." he gurgled. "... Better now..."

I helped him sit up. He was sweating and dark rims were starting to form under his eyes; for once he didn't look as if he thought life was one big party.

"Don't do it," I said. "It's too dangerous."

"Do you have a better idea?" he asked.

I looked around. By now most of the cave floor was underwater, and the water was still rising. If we stayed here, we might not even have time to die of hunger. We would probably drown first. And Aunt Isa, Mrs Pommerans, Shanaia, Kahla's dad and Mr Malkin... They would drown too, wouldn't they? Even zombies needed oxygen. We could always try sitting them up against the rock wall, but what if the water level rose higher than that? I looked up at the stalactite ceiling and the small wedge of daylight. It was our only way out.

"No," I said quietly. "I don't have a better idea."

Oscar got up.

"Move, peasant," he said in his best dictator voice – which wasn't very convincing. "And let the master of the universe show that climbing wall who's boss."

I was pretty sure he was bruised all over and I could see that the scratches on his right hand were bleeding. I was also pretty sure that he had no wish at all to climb up the wall and risk falling yet again. This wasn't something he was doing to show off or to win a competition. He was doing it because it was the only way he could save all of us.

"Oscar?"

"Yes, peasant?"

"I think you're super-cool. And don't you dare fall again, do you hear me?"

He grinned across his whole freckled face, clicked his heels and saluted me like a tin soldier.

"Yes, milady," he said. "Now get out of my way. This time I'll make it all the way up, just you wait and see!"

A small leap took him to the first ledge and he carried on quickly, without hesitation, up to a gap where he could wedge in most of his body. Then he reached the tricky place where he'd fallen the first time. But he'd learned from experience – his hand into one crack, his foot there, and his knee on a narrow rock shelf, a firm grip on the stalactite, swing himself round, right foot up...

He was nearly at the top. He disappeared behind a protrusion and I stopped being able to watch his every move, I could only hear his laboured breathing and the scraping of feet, hands, clothes, elbows and knees against the cliff wall. I held my breath. If he slipped and tumbled down now...

But he didn't.

"I'm the master of the universe!" I heard from above – somewhat out of breath and maybe not quite the lion roar he was hoping for. But he was up.

It would be wrong to say that it was plain sailing from there on. Even with the help of an old lawn-mower tractor and some ropes Oscar found in the garden shed at Westmark, it was still a challenge to hoist the stiff and uncooperative bodies up through the narrow light shaft. Handling them as if they were plastic dolls was weird. I discovered that it was possible to move their arms and legs, bend a knee, extend an elbow, which made it a little easier to get them up and out. But it also enhanced the sensation that they were dolls. And the water continued to rise, so towards the end I was wading around up to my knees in cold water. But we got them up, all five of them, and finally it was my turn to slip my legs through the improvised harness we'd made and be pulled up through the well.

"The tractor was a really good idea," I said to Oscar when I was finally back on the grass, in the wind and the sun outside the wall that surrounded Westmark.

"Well, they're heavy," Oscar said. "Heavier than us. I'd worked out that we wouldn't be able to pull them up ourselves."

Aunt Isa was lying on the grass, staring up at the sky with open eyes. I wanted to close them, but I didn't because it felt like something you did to a dead person. Mrs Pommerans was lying next to her, with one arm sticking straight up into the air. Mr Malkin...

"Hang on," I said. "What's that?"

Because Mr Malkin wasn't quite as immobile as the others. Something stirred, approximately where his heart was. And suddenly a tiny nose poked out of his waistcoat pocket, and a pair of shiny black beady eyes peered at the sun. It was the baby dormouse. I had completely forgotten it was there.

"Wow, fancy it surviving all of that..." Oscar said. "What a supermouse, eh?"

"It's actually not a mouse," I said.

"OK, then a... didn't he call it a dormouse?"

"Yes. It'll grow quite a lot bigger than a mouse, and its tail is bushy, almost like a squirrel's."

"I still think it's a supermouse," Oscar said quietly, holding his hand out to the dormouse. "It's wearing a mask and everything, can't you see? I bet it has a secret identity."

He was right about the mask. Unlike the common dormice Aunt Isa often had hibernating in baskets or shoeboxes on the bookcase, this one seemed to have a black band stretching from its eyes and across its cheeks.

"We have to take it with us," I said. "Mr Malkin can't look after it now."

Oscar looked down at the lifeless bodies. "Is there really nothing you can do to... bring them back to life?"

"If there was, don't you think I would've done it?"

My voice was harsh and angry, and Oscar took a step back.

"Relax," he said. "I wasn't trying to hassle you."

"No, I know." I was trying really hard to calm down, but everything inside me was whirling around. My head felt like a cement mixer, and my stomach wasn't much better. My emotions were all jumbled up, there was relief that we'd escaped and brought the others up with us, helplessness because I hadn't done a better job, fear that Aunt Isa and her friends would die here, all staring eyes and rigid zombie bodies. Guilt. Grief. Loss. I wanted Aunt Isa to wake up and help us. I wanted Cat to come back. I wanted everything to be better than it was.

"It's my fault," I whispered. "I called them. They came to help me – and now they're just lying there."

"How about Thuja?" Oscar said. "The Raven Mothers? Do you think they'll know how to wake them up?"

"We have to ask them," I said. "But... I can't find my way to Raven Kettle on my own. I can't even find my way home." The cement mixer feeling worsened.

Oscar looked at me glumly.

"My mum is going to go ape," he said.

I don't know why, but hearing that made me feel a bit better. Perhaps because it reminded me that the ordinary world still existed. Oscar's mum was out there somewhere. As were my own mum, and my dad.

The problem was just how to find them again.

Then I heard flapping as if a big, clumsy bird was trying to fly past us. I looked up, but I couldn't see anything. Not until I heard someone sneeze, and I turned around.

"I'b so bery, bery sorry," The Nothing said and sniffled. Her dust mite allergy was clearly in full flow. "I *know* I promised to stay at home and look after Bumble, but... I got so lonely, and it's so hard not to follow someone..." Then she spotted Aunt Isa and the others. "Oh no, oh dear. What happened to them?"

I made no reply. I just grabbed the small, snuffling bird girl and hugged her tight until she started to squirm because I was hurting her.

CHAPTER NINETEEN

The Ninth Life

"Where's Isa?" my mum demanded to know. "Did she just abandon you?"

"Mum," I said. "You're not listening. She didn't abandon us. She saved me. And now... now I have to save her."

Mum was standing in the middle of Aunt Isa's living room wearing her coat and with raindrops in her hair. Dad was still in hospital; the doctors wanted to carry out a few more tests before they discharged him.

"It was me who brought us back," The Nothing said proudly. "I remembered the whole way. The whole way!"

"Yes," I said. "We'd have been lost without you."

Mum took a deep breath.

"Are you telling me that Isa won't be back for a while?"

"She'll be back as soon as I work out how to help her," I said stubbornly. We'd had to leave Aunt Isa and the others at Westmark. It simply wasn't possible to bring them home on the wildways. Oscar and I had made a kind of stretcher from an old sun lounger and we'd managed to carry Aunt Isa and the others inside the house. We'd dragged beds down to the hall because it was easier than heaving deadweight adults up a lot of stairs. I didn't know if it helped them. I wasn't sure that they were aware of the difference. But I felt better when I saw them lying almost normally in their beds, as if they were just ill and not... sleeping zombies. Leaving them, however, felt completely and utterly wrong, and I welled up with rage when Mum talked about Aunt Isa as if she were completely irresponsible, when the truth was that she and the others had given their... lives, pretty much, to save me and Oscar.

I'd tried explaining it to her, but it was as if Mum didn't *want* to understand what had happened.

"They'll wake up again, I guess," she'd said, as if they were just taking an afternoon nap. And it got the cement mixer in my head and my stomach going again because I wasn't sure that they ever would wake up – not unless I helped them. Or found someone who could.

"What a mess," Mum sounded irritated.

"Mum, it's not as if she did it on purpose!"

"No, I don't suppose she did. But what about the animals? The horse and the goats and Bumble?"

"I'll take care of them. Me and The Nothing."

Mum looked at me as if I'd suddenly turned into some strange creature she'd never seen before.

"Clara Mouse," she said. "I'm trying to be patient here, I really am. But this is... this is insane. You're twelve years old—"

"Thirteen!"

"Thirteen years old. You must be out of your mind if you think you can live here on your own until Aunt Isa comes back."

"If I can't live here alone, then you'll have to stay here too. Or Dad. But she's your sister. Doesn't that count for something?"

Oscar looked from one of us to the other. I think he was relieved that his own mum wasn't here as well. He would have enough on his plate once he got home. Not least explaining away the small, living bump in his shirt pocket. To my enormous surprise it was Oscar who'd tempted the dormouse out of its hiding place in Mr Malkin's pocket. Perhaps it liked the idea of being a supermouse with a secret identity – at any rate, it had darted willingly into Oscar's shirt pocket and settled down there.

"What about school?" Mum said. "You can't just stay away. Have you thought about that?"

"I can be off sick," I said. "Look. I was bitten by a leech. It's very serious, and I won't be able to go back until after the summer holidays. But Oscar has promised to ring me and let me know what our homework is, so I don't fall too far behind."

"Clara!"

"Mum, don't you get it?" My voice grew thin and shrill, and I had to take a couple of deep breaths. She would pay closer attention if I didn't get "hysterical", as she called it, when I got angry. "I'm sorry that you're upset," I said as calmly as I could. "But I'm not coming home with you. If you make me, then I'll run away. This is more important than school. It's more important than me. More important than you, as it happens. I might be only thirteen years old, but when you're a wildwitch it's the same as being a grown-up. And you know it."

It was as if something inside her cracked. She looked around as if she couldn't quite believe that she was standing here arguing with me like this. She pushed her wet fringe aside with impatient fingers, and then she suddenly stuck out an arm and pulled me close.

"I don't want to fight with you," she said. "Come home. We'll work something out."

I snuggled up to her, but I didn't give in.

"I don't want to fight with you either," I said. "Please, just stay *here* for a week? You can work from here just as well as from home, can't you?"

"A week," she said tentatively. "And then we go home?"

I considered it. The Nothing wasn't sure that she could find the way to Raven Kettle along the wildways. If I had to travel there without her help, how long would it take me? And what if Thuja and the Raven Mothers couldn't help Aunt Isa and the others?

"I can't promise you that," I said. "I don't know if one week is enough."

The Nothing started flapping her wings, happy that we were no longer fighting.

"Tea?" she said. "Would you like me to make some tea?"

"No, thank you," Mum said. "I need to drive Oscar home and pick up Clara's dad from the hospital. And I guess I'd better pack some clothes and schoolbooks for the return journey. And my laptop."

My aching body relaxed with relief.

"I'd like some tea, please," I said to The Nothing.

Mum touched my scorched eyebrows carefully.

"How about we take you to the hospital?" she said.

"No need," I said. "Aunt Isa has an ointment that..." I ground to a halt because the words reminded me of the strange, rigid Aunt Isa doll now lying in a bed at Westmark, still with her eyes wide open. "It's very good for burns," I mumbled.

"One week," Mum said. "That's all I've promised!"

"Yes."

When Mum and Oscar had driven off in the Volvo with its new windscreen, I stood for a while in the living room not knowing quite what to do with myself. It was odd, Aunt Isa not being there. Bumble, too, seemed at a loss, although he was pleased to see me. The Nothing flipped between being proud as a peacock and totally down in the dumps, and I had to praise her over and over again for having been so brave and so clever.

Although it was noon, Hoot-Hoot came sweeping through the open bedroom window on silent wings. Perhaps he was restless because he could feel that something was wrong with Aunt Isa.

"Oh, Hoot-Hoot." I held up my arm and he actually landed on it. He looked at me with glowing orange eyes and made a clicking, almost questioning, sound. "I promise I'll bring her home," I said to him, but right there and then I felt so despondent that I hardly dared believe it myself. Aunt Isa. Shanaia. Lovely Mrs Pommerans. Mr Malkin. And Kahla's dad...

Kahla. Kahla knew nothing. She was probably stuck at home – wherever that was, she never really talked about it, but it was probably somewhere warm – waiting for her dad to come back.

"Nothing?"

"Yes?"

"Did Aunt Isa ever send messages with Hoot-Hoot to Kahla's dad?"

"Yes. If anything came up or there was too much snow. He knows the way."

"Good. Do you know where to find a pen and some paper?"

I wrote a brief message to Kahla. I didn't tell her what had happened to her dad because it wasn't something you could write on a scrap of paper small enough to tie around Hoot-Hoot's leg. I just said she had to come. Hoot-Hoot tolerated my fumbling fingers attaching the message with a bit of twine. An elastic band would have been easier, but I was afraid that would be too tight.

"Kahla," I said to him, while making an effort to visualize her in my mind: dark eyes, cinnamon skin and at least two colourful hats... "Find Kahla."

He chirped at me. Shook his head once, a lightning quick movement that blurred his feathers before they settled. Then he flapped his wings vigorously a couple of times and swooped out through the window.

"Do you think he understood me?" I said to The Nothing.

"Why wouldn't he?" she said, and looked genuinely baffled.

I was exhausted. I could barely stay upright. I drank the tea The Nothing had made, then lay down on the sofa and covered myself with a blanket. I had to get some sleep. When Kahla turned up – *if* she turned up and Hoot-Hoot hadn't just flown off to catch himself a water vole or two – then together we would find the way to Raven Kettle. I had to believe that.

"Cat?" I whispered without holding out much hope. He was gone. He'd disappeared in an explosion of fire, blood and bones. I think that was why I'd given my mum such a hard time. Stood my ground. Once I got back to Mercury Street, I wouldn't be able to just nip down to the wildways because he wouldn't be there to help me. That was why I had to stay here.

And yet I got an answer. A sudden heat wrapped itself around my leg.

Yes.

I flung open my eyes. He was lying on top of the blanket, looking at me with his neon-yellow eyes. He looked smaller and older. His fur wasn't as raven-black as it used to be. Nor were his ears as upright; instead they stuck out to the side, a little flat, and his tail lay still, not even the tip was flicking. If it

hadn't been that Cat was never tired, then I would have said he was exhausted.

"Cat! I thought..." I thought you were dead. I didn't say it out loud.

This is the last time, he said.

"What do you mean? The last time..."

I've no more lives left. Nine lives must be spread very thin to span more than four hundred years.

His voice already sounded a little alien. More like Viridian's than his own.

"So you're... Nightclaw?"

Among other things.

"But you said... you said that you were.... that I was yours." Stupid, monumentally stupid, to lie here being jealous of a wildwitch who had been pretty much dead for four centuries. But jealous was exactly what I was. He had to love me more than her, a childish little voice whispered inside me. Yet at the same time, I knew that cats don't love you. They stay with you for as long as they please. He'd stayed with me, and now he was ready to move on. He might have stayed – perhaps he could have stayed, if my hesitation in the cave hadn't cost him his second-to-last life. Or was it his last?

"Am I not yours any more?" I asked, barely able to steady my voice.

He walked on soft cat paws across me and the blanket and licked my forehead, where the scars from his claws had turned into pale, white, almost invisible lines.

You're your own person, he said. And then he disappeared as quietly as if he'd never been there, and the warmth and the weight of his body were nothing but a dream.

I cried for a bit, but not for as long as I wanted to. I was too tired and everything hurt. I lay on the sofa, listening to the rain, dozing off and waiting. The rain got denser, heavier and noisier, and my body got even stiffer and sorer than it already was.

The Nothing came flapping over a couple of times, worried and anxious, and I couldn't comfort her properly.

Now I knew what it was like to lose a wildfriend. Now I knew what Shanaia had gone through; indeed what Kimmie had experienced before she became Chimera. I was hurt. I felt empty. There was a void inside I couldn't fill.

I stayed on that sofa for hours. Mum didn't come back. Kahla didn't turn up. But then something... something else happened.

I sat up with a jerk. The blanket slid to the floor, and I had to push off against the coffee table before I could stand up.

"What is it?" The Nothing asked.

"There's something out there," I said. "By the door."

"I can't hear anything."

Bumble had got up from his basket. His tail wagged decisively, and he was whining in his excited "hello friend!" mode.

I opened the door. And in marched an adolescent kitten, black with white paws, soaking wet and scrawny, and yet in no way a beggar. It looked up at me with yellow eyes and meowed silently so I could see its sharp white teeth and its pink mouth. It had already moved in, that much was clear, though less than a minute had passed and it hadn't said a word.

I opened a tin of mackerel and tipped the contents onto a saucer. The kitten attacked the food as soon as I put the saucer on the floor, and wolfed it down in less than a minute. Then it strolled back into the living room, jumped onto the sofa and fell asleep.

It wasn't Cat. It wasn't the same. Cat had been big, strong and magical, and had taken care of me. This was quite the reverse – I'd have to take care of Kitten, and he had just as much to learn from me as I from him. And yet just like that my mood had completely changed.

I knew I would find the Raven Mothers, with or without Kahla. I knew we would save Aunt Isa, Shanaia and the others. Everything would be all right. I gently stroked the Kitten across his skinny black back, and he opened his eyes slightly – just a tiny sliver of yellow.

"Are you mine now?" I asked. "Are you my wild-friend?"

He just closed his eyes again. But somewhere inside me there was a tiny, meowing voice; it was low and weak and hard to understand, but even so I thought I knew what he was trying to tell me.

Mine... he whispered.

THE WILDWITCH
STORY SO FAR...

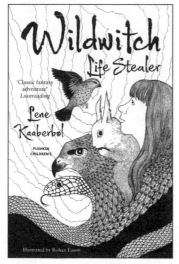